"In *I-5*, Summer Brenner deals with the onerous and gruesome subject of sex trafficking calmly and forcefully, making the reader feel the pain of its victims. The trick to forging a successful narrative is always in the details, and *I-5* provides them in abundance. This book bleeds truth – after you finish it, the blood will be on your hands." ∼ BARRY GIFFORD, AUTHOR OF *WILD AT HEART* AND THE *SAILOR AND LULA* SERIES, SCREENPLAYS FOR FILMS DIRECTED BY DAVID LYNCH AND MATT DILLON, AND FORMER EDITOR OF BLACK LIZARD BOOKS.

"Insightful, innovative and riveting. After its lyrical beginning inside Anya's head, *I-5* shifts momentum into a rollicking gangsters-on-the-lam tale that is in turns blackly humorous, suspenseful, heart-breaking and always populated by intriguing characters. Anya is a wonderful, believable heroine, her tragic tale told from the inside out, without a shred of sentimental pity, which makes it all the stronger. A twisty, fast-paced ride you won't soon forget." ∼ DENISE HAMILTON, EDITOR OF *LOS ANGELES NOIR*, AUTHOR OF THE EDGAR AWARD NOMINATED EVE DIAMOND NOVELS AND *L.A. TIMES* BESTSELLER, *THE LAST EMBRACE*.

"I'm in awe. *I-5* moves so fast you can barely catch your breath. It's as tough as tires, as real and nasty as road rage, and best of all, it careens at breakneck speed over as many twists and turns as you'll find on The Grapevine. What a ride! *I-5*'s a hard-boiled standout." ∼ JULIE SMITH, EDITOR OF *NEW ORLEANS NOIR* AND AUTHOR OF THE *SKIP LANGDON* AND *TALBA WALLIS* CRIME NOVEL SERIES.

"Summer Brenner has written a novel that will beat you up – chances are you deserve it. *I-5* cuts through layers of flesh to reveal the true heart of noir: that for every American dream there are a thousand nightmares. I have read no better novel in the genre. Roll over Williford, tell Goodis the news." ∼ OWEN HILL, AUTHOR OF *THE INCREDIBLE DOUBLE* AND *THE CHANDLER APARTMENTS*, ALONG WITH SIX POETRY CHAPBOOKS AND A BOOK OF SHORT FICTION. HE HAS BEEN A BUYER AT MOE'S BOOKS IN BERKELEY FOR TWENTY-TWO YEARS.

"Summer Brenner provides an insider's look at the seedy world of sexual slavery that shifts young girls across oceans to fulfill insatiable yearnings of greed and lust. Nothing gets sugar-coated, yet Brenner shows sincere sympathy and warmth for her characters. I found it hard to stop turning the pages until I might learn whether Anya can make it to safety." ∾ DAVID BATSTONE, AUTHOR OF *NOT FOR SALE*, PRESIDENT OF THE NOT FOR SALE CAMPAIGN.

"Familiar yet unfamiliar, Brenner takes the reader on a journey marred with sex and crime that exposes the harsh reality of the invisibility of women, immigrants and the marginalized, struggling to survive." ∾ OPAL PALMER ADISA, AUTHOR OF *UNTIL JUDGMENT COMES, EROS MUSE, CARIBBEAN PASSION, IT BEGINS WITH TEARS,* AND *BAKE-FACE AND OTHER GUAVA STORIES.* SHE IS A PROFESSOR AT CALIFORNIA COLLEGE OF THE ARTS.

Other Books
by Summer Brenner

∾

FICTION
The Missing Lover
Ivy, Tale of a Homeless Girl in San Francisco
Presque nulle part
One Minute Movies
Dancers and the Dance
The Soft Room

POETRY
From the Heart to the Center
Everyone Came Dressed as Water

AUDIO
Arundo Salon, "Because the Spirit Moved"

Excerpts of a version of this novel appeared as "Elsa" in the online magazine, *Exquisite Corpse*, edited by Andrei Codrescu.

A word of appreciation to Vassili Goloubev for his great help in researching Anya's life in Russia. Many thanks to friends and family who read the manuscript: Ella Baff, Joanna Bean, Gillian Boal, Iain Boal, Jim Brook, Linda Norton, Amelie Prescott, Karl Roeseler, and Jane White; and Laura Blake Peterson at Curtis Brown, Ltd.

All eyes on her; proboscis twisted,
Hoof, whisker, bushy-crested tail,
Horn, blood-red tongue, all lash and flail,
And arms unfleshed and bony-fisted
All point and rampantly entwine
With one great roar: She's mine! She's mine!

Eugene Onegin
BY ALEXANDER PUSHKIN
TRANSLATION BY WALTER ARNDT

I-5
A Novel of Crime,
Transport, and Sex

SWITCHBLADE

switch·blade (swĭch´blād´) n.
a different slice of hardboiled fiction where the dreamers and the schemers, the dispossessed and the damned, and the hobos and the rebels tango at the edge of society.

I-5

SUMMER BRENNER

*A Novel of Crime,
Transport, and Sex*

PM PRESS

I-5: A Novel of Crime, Transport, and Sex
By Summer Brenner

Copyright © 2009 Summer Brenner
This edition copyright © 2009 PM Press
All Rights Reserved

Published by:
PM Press
PO Box 23912
Oakland, CA 94623
www.pmpress.org

Cover Illustration by Roderick Constance © 2009 www.shadowshapes.com
Designed by Courtney Utt

ISBN: 978-1-60486-019-1
Library Of Congress Control Number: 2008909318
10 9 8 7 6 5 4 3 2 1

Printed in the USA on recycled paper.

Written
as a curse
on them that
force women
and girls
into bondage

1

Outside, Anya can distinguish three different kinds of noise. One is a bird near her window. Except for early morning, this one is silent all day.

The second are the sirens of the city. No matter where she is, day and night, she hears them. She attracts them like a magnet. As they approach, they get shriller and louder. Once they are near, they sound like bombs falling on her head. As they start to fade, the silence grows stunning and absolute.

The third is a mystery. It positions itself faithfully at the corner of the street and never leaves. Faithfully, it chirps day and night in alternating tones, tones that travel in distinct but opposite directions. One chirp is like a mechanical cuckoo, the other a hollow suction.

Anya knows the noises well. She has listened to them for several days. She understands the first two, but the third baffles her. She cannot understand something that makes the same two unnatural sounds at precisely the same intervals. This is new to her experience.

She tries to fathom its mission. If it's a bird, it does not sing for the joy of morning, for its song is uttered at all hours. If it's inspired by pain, that she understands. But any bird, any living creature, eventually tires. Pain is tiring. You can only cry out for so long. You sob until you're wrenched and wrung, but then you stop.

This thing almost never tires. It almost never sleeps. She cannot imagine what affliction or ecstasy it contains, but it is torture to her.

More tortuous than sirens. Sirens she has heard all her life. She knows goose-honks from screeches, ambulances from fire trucks, fire trucks from police cars. These sorts of songs signal emergencies, rare in peace, constant in war. She is familiar with both frequencies.

Anya lies in bed awake although it is late. She is tired and anxious. The anxiety doesn't let her sleep. When she dozes, the mysterious little caw disturbs her. She loathes its idiotic repetitions. She feels besieged. She dreams of killing it. She hopes it's as small as a sparrow and can be crushed by hand. She stretches her fingers in their joints, back and forth. She is warming her joints like a pianist. She must keep her hands strong if she is to succeed at killing the sound that has become her greatest torment.

Anya has been in this room for four days. She hasn't left. She's on leave. She can lie in bed as long as she wants. She can watch television. She can listen to the radio. She can read newspapers and magazines in English and Russian. She can bathe many times a day.

However, she is not permitted to go outside. She is locked in the room. She cannot see out because the windows are covered and the glass painted black. She has been taken to the room blindfolded. She has been taken in a car. She probably traveled for two days before she arrived. She isn't sure. She was drugged and sleeping through most of the trip. Whenever she awoke, she was given a sandwich, drink, banana, piece of candy, and another sleeping pill. Whatever she asked for *within reason*, she was given.

Anya can do whatever she wants, *within reason*. They bring her newspapers in Russian. They know she likes to read. They want her to rest and relax. She will be on leave for a day or two more so she can relax. They want her to recover. They have told her she's too skinny. They say she doesn't eat enough. They think she's working too hard. They bring her milkshakes and bananas.

Always bananas and chocolate. They bring her joints to make her hungry. They say they can't make her eat, but eating is a glorious part of life. They like to say persuasive things. They like to make themselves sound philosophical.

They also fancy the phrase, *in principle*. They elevate themselves with *in principle*. They employ such phrases for emphasis. They can say anything as long as they add a touch of loftiness. When they speak in such ways, it is without irony.

They say, "You should get on your fucking knees and crawl across the room." And when they add *in principle* to their propositions, it lends them an air of dignity: as if *in principle* all mankind has been waiting to do their bidding.

Every evening they come into the room and say, "Anya, here is bread. Here is soup. Eat, Anya. Eating is a splendid part of life."

They laugh when they say such things and slurp down the soup. They've brought enough for themselves. They've brought enough for a dozen. They throw themselves on the food. They throw napkins, drinks, cartons of food around Anya's room.

They offer her vodka. That, she takes. She can hardly wait for the vodka. She drinks it over ice in a short bar glass. She doesn't like the sleeping pills, but she loves the vodka and the way it makes her body slip inside a smooth dream.

After one glass of iced vodka, Anya is content. After two, she almost laughs. At least, she is ready to smile. But if she has three glasses, she cries. She can't stop crying. Nothing consoles her. That's why she is strictly limited.

They don't leave her the bottle. They don't leave it behind. That is not within reason, they tell her. They do not want her to become an alcoholic.

"Like every fucking whore in Russia," they say.

Then, they laugh. They're jolly, they are. They rarely miss an opportunity to eat and drink and laugh. They like Anya. They want her to join in. They want her to party with them, but she tells them she's on vacation.

She wants to be alone, she says. And they accept that. First, they consult. Then, they accept that it's within reason.

2

The radio is turned on next to the bed. The bedside lamp is on too. Only artificial light illuminates the room. Anya is accustomed to thin, cool light. When she's working, she rarely goes out. When she's on leave, she might go out but only accompanied. Sometimes she stays indoors for weeks. She no longer cares if she goes out or not.

When she first arrived, she was required to stay inside for four weeks. They said it was to help her acclimate. She lived in one room without windows. She named it her cocoon. She called herself a pupa in a cocoon. She told herself she was lucky to find such a silky, protective covering. She coached herself on how to keep steady and not lose her chance, whatever it took.

She suppressed any regrets. After all, what should she regret? That she exchanged an old hole for a new one? At least, the plumbing was now reliable. In fact, she considers it significant progress, for in transport alone she has relocated from one continent across the ocean to another. Above everything else, that was the glorious promise.

When Anya emerged at the end of the initiation period, she was surprised what made her cry out with recognition. Most of all, it was the sun. When she looked up and saw the sun, she cried. For the first time, she perceived that light, like water, is capable of permeating everything. Every color, shape, shadow, and reflection receives its singular definition solely because of light. She cried because like everyone, she used to take so much for granted.

Now Anya understands why people worship the sun. Someday when she is asked her religion, she will say "sun-worshiper."

The tribute to Dakota Staton has been interrupted by the news. Anya only half-listens. There is a war somewhere with casualties. A dozen, a thousand, a hundred-thousand innocents?

Innocent? She hates the word. Innocent is a shield for the guilty. It is certain they who decry the fate of the innocent are guilty too. The news makes her smirk. Anya takes a pinch of pride in having swiftly moved from victim to casualty to survivor. That's over now. Past.

She gets out of bed and trips past the card table and four matching chairs, the poorly upholstered love-seat. Leave is almost over. They have warned her.

She checks the door just in case. She checks the closet just in case. On the floor is a large valise, filled mostly with underwear and gowns. Her raincoat and wool jacket hang next to a couple of silky synthetic dresses. Her shoes – mules, sandals, high boots, sneakers – tumble in disarray next to the valise. At least, they allow her to have shoes. She grabs a pair of thick cotton socks and pads into the bathroom.

In the mirror somewhere is her face. It looks hard to her. The same but hard like a mold created for the sculpture of a woman. No doubt a beauty in her youth, now recaptured for perpetuity in metal, stone, or something cheap like plaster.

Anya examines her nose. It's big but not bad. The big nose balances her big tits. Actually, the nose is long rather than big, which in her case makes the same impression. The nostrils, however, are disproportionately small, tense, and shapely. They always look flared. Her lips are thin but elastic. They stretch easily like rubber bands. The teeth are bad. That cannot be helped. There was a dentist but no one went to him. Once there was an emergency and she went. He pulled one of her molars. The bottom row of teeth is crooked. They're yellowed from coffee and unfiltered cigarettes, but she has given up both. She's on a health kick.

"Within reason," she mutters, half-smiling.

The skin too cannot be helped. A few pock marks are visible by the temples and a couple more on her left cheek. That's why she habitually shows the right side of her face. She lives in profile. Sometimes they call her the Hieroglyphic. It goes well with their other nickname, Anya the Egyptian.

The skin color is worse than the texture. It ranges from sallow to olive. It always looks slightly wet, slightly feverish, and sweat beads easily on her upper lip and forehead. If her hair shade is too light or too brassy, then she looks nearly green. Their other nicknames for her are Seaweed and Mermaid. They like to tease her, which is normally better than a beating. However, sometimes she wishes she never had to hear their voices again. Sometimes she'd prefer the strap.

She strives for dark ash blond. Too much yellow gives her hair a greenish cast like verdigris. There is also the additional pallor that comes from living indoors under artificial light. The women who work long hours in factories under fluorescent tubes have the same coloring. Even when their skin is dark, the epidermis looks sickly.

Anya's eyes are good. No one disputes that. They're speckled and green, large, deep-set, and shrewd. Besides the color, they slant upward and give a Eurasian cast to her face. A blond Mongol. Such exotica only takes a stray drop of blood and a bottle of dye.

However, her eyes have lost a quantity of liveliness. That's to be expected. In measurable quantities, life drains the liveliness out of a person. She knows that well. She remembers her mother's eyes. Eventually, the life force behind the sockets disappeared.

Aside from any color, the texture of hair is excellent. It's wavy and thick. It's shoulder-length, which is both convenient and chic. Wherever she is, someone is hired to come in and cut her hair. Every six weeks, it's cut. The price varies, but like everything, it goes on her tab. $75 plus tip is average.

Her eyebrows, she shaves off. Once they were calico and as furry as caterpillars. Now she prefers them smooth and brown. She expertly pencils them on, and whenever they're altogether missing, the bare, denuded protrusions above her eyes accentuate the broad, Slavic shape of her head. Missing eyebrows is like shaved pubic hair. It's unexpected but conveys its own allure.

Scattered across the commode are tubes of lipstick, mostly dark like dried blood. The color accentuates the discoloration of her teeth, but she fancies a lurid mood. It goes well with her eyebrows and suggests something mischievous and forbidden.

In a row behind the sink are tins of rouge to hide or lift her pasty skin to rosy. She squeezes her cheeks until they bruise. Then, she brushes her entire face with powder before she draws on her eyebrows. She prefers lilac eye shadow and dark-blue mascara, but today on leave, she forgoes both.

Next to the sink is a jewelry box. She favors gold and pearls. She owns one strand of champagne cultured pearls, but the other assortment of dangling earrings, studs, bangles, cuff bracelets, chokers, and long chains are costume.

Anya drops her Victoria Secret jacquard robe to the floor. She examines the front of her body. The moles trip across her stomach like mouse turds. She counts them. There is one more than before. Twelve mouse turds instead of eleven. Is it cancer? She picks at the new mole until it bleeds. Can she make it cancer?

Music has returned to the little box by the bed. It's the sweet, reedy voice of Chet Baker. His voice used to make her cry because it sounded so girlish, weeping and giggling inside the body of a man. The hermaphrodite's voice could pull her over the edge with its regret, but she is beyond regret too. Victim, casualty, survivor, and no regrets.

Anya's time is almost up. They've told her after the next assignment, she will have earned her liberty. *Liberty* is the word they use. *Liberty* fits the way they elevate their role to a cause. Regarding Anya, they say it's *within reason* now. Her debt is nearly paid off.

Anya glances behind her. As usual, she is struck by the curves she rarely sees. They are likely the best part of her. Her legs are long, the muscles well-defined from walking into the hills throughout her youth. Her legs show off well in heels, short skirts, and baby-doll pajamas.

They were hills with gradual inclines that went up and behind the town. After climbing a kilometer of rocky, unpaved road, you reached a plateau with the best view of the valley. From one end to the other, a lazy river wound its way around.

Anya's grandparents had a farm on the plateau, and for years Anya traveled every day by foot to visit. In 1992, their farm was wrecked by the crash of a small military plane. Then afterwards, her grandmother Baba died from falling into one of the holes the plane made. The doctors called it, "Complications from a fall," but Anya thought the complications were much larger. After all, why was there a hole instead of a farm?

3

Because of the view, Anya continued to walk up to Baba's farm. When she had her first boyfriend, they took a quilt and stored it in what remained of the *senoval*. There was still enough hay to lie on but in the spring of their pubescent courtship, they went outside into a field of wild onions in the ruins of Baba's garden. Or lay on a haystack in an adjacent field watching stars. When it rained, they went back inside.

Thinking of Baba makes Anya extremely happy, extremely sad. Anya answers to Baba like some people answer to God. She has a habit of writing to her. *Dear Ba, Pray for me.* It's easier to write and lie to a dead person. Then, they don't worry. If she wrote to her mother or old boyfriend, she's sure they'd worry. She doesn't want to lie to the living. However, any correspondence is censored before it's mailed so their worry would only be intuitive. A vibration sent halfway around the world contained inside the words. All lies.

Every month they make Anya write a letter home. They give her something to copy. They say it goes out with the money order. They remind her she's working to help her family in Russia. The letters are always the same. *I am working hard, and that is good. I love America. I am working so you can come here too. Soon I'll be moving so it's better not to write to me. I'll write you soon. I love and miss you but I am happy.* That's what they make her write, *I'm happy.*

At the beginning she refused to write. She said she wasn't a liar.

That got a big laugh. "A whore but not a liar," they repeated. They hit her with a belt across her calves like a bad child. Then, she agreed to write.

Dear Ba, Pray for me. Anya always writes on Sundays. She always starts her letters the same way. She herself is not a religious person, but Baba was religious. Devout. She had an icon where she burned her candles. She burned them for the living and the dead. She burned them if she had hopes or desires. She always burnt candles for Anya. "Anechka," she called her. She told Anya that Jesus had blessed her. When she was small, Anya did feel blessed. Now she thinks it was Baba herself who was the blessing.

Anya likes to recall the candles by the icon, the smell of melting wax. Soft and pliable like caramel. Her favorite candy was the caramel roosters on sticks, *petushok na palochke.* Anya remembers the bowls of strawberries Ba would leave by her bed. When she was a little girl, she would wake in the summer morning late, still sleepy because the nights were filled with light. She couldn't go to sleep until midnight. She slept long, past the time for breakfast. She would wake to find wild strawberries on a small blue saucer, as blue as a flower or the sky. She never heard or saw Ba put them there. Baba told her *dobraja feja* brought it. The blue plate, the strawberries.

Dear Ba, Pray for me. She often writes to Ba about food. She misses the food from the garden. She misses the fresh onions, tomatoes, and mushrooms from the woods cooked with fried potatoes. Sometimes she writes and complains about her mother Oksana, Ba's daughter. Sometimes she blames her mother for everything. Ba would tell her that was normal. When you can't face yourself, you blame others. That's what Ba would say. Ba was wise in some ways. And stupid too. But it doesn't matter. She loved Ba's stupid gossip and repetitions, her foul breath. In fact, Anya has come to realize that love is defined by loving what you dislike in someone else. She hopes someday to meet someone she loves more than hates.

After she writes the letters, she puts them by the bed. They tell her they will mail the letters. She has given them the address of the farm. She has told them her grandmother is alive. They commend her for writing to her Baba. Anya is proud of her penmanship. She is proud of her English too. Of course, she writes in Russian, but she can now translate almost everything she wants to say.

Anya smiles warmly at the mirror. Her lips widen nearly to her ears, break her face into two yellowish halves like a grapefruit. She mouths the word, Ba. One syllable like the sound a baby animal makes. In English too, they say Ma and Pa.

"Ba, Ba, Ba," Anya says. She knows she must be good. She must be patient. She has waited long. She has worked hard. She must wait only a little longer.

4

Anya hears a large animate object knock against the outside door of the room. She hears fumbling and jangling. Reflexively, she tenses.

"Fuck," the familiar voice says. No hostility, only inconvenience.

Suddenly, it leaves the range of Anya's hearing. When it returns, she hears a collection of keys brush the escutcheon. There is another hushed curse. Then, the keys are inserted into two keyholes: one door lock and one bolt.

"You here?" A thick, disembodied voice calls.

"Where else the fuck would I be?" She responds from the bathroom.

"Cheerful," the masculine voice is deep and energetic.

"Tired," Anya whines.

"Too much time off," he chides.

Marty lumbers over to the small loveseat. He lands rather than sits on its unresponsive foam cushion. He brushes the lapels of his misshapen tweed jacket. He lets his small hands fall onto his bulky thighs. He examines his fingernails. Then, he takes the corner of a matchbook and cleans them.

Wrapped tightly in her red rayon jacquard robe, Anya emerges from the bathroom. Her hair is wet and brushed back. Her face is refreshed and almost clear. She looks her age, which is twenty-three.

Marty is struck and surprised by her youthful, wholesome

appearance. His fingers fold together in approval.

"Isn't it too fucking early to fucking visit?" she asks.

Even her foul expletive language strikes him as youthful. She could almost be American.

"Hey, watch fuck language," he is good-naturedly compelled to say.

She shrugs and lights an extra long, filter-tipped blond tobacco cigarette. The unpleasant filter is part of her new health regime.

"I brought you fresh orange juice." Marty holds out a paper cup with a plastic lid. "From Farmers' Market."

"Farmers' what? Where the fuck are we?"

"Go on, it's good for you. Good for complexion," he winces about Anya's skin. It's a shame, he thinks, but then so many things are.

Anya takes a tiny sip. Only a few drops of nectar reach her tongue, but that's sufficient. The sensation rushes from the tongue to her brain. She had clearly forgotten, but the tongue still faithfully recalls.

A soldier with oranges and a makeshift press in his rucksack intercepted Anya on a road. He had carried the oranges around for a week, thinking to save them for a desperate moment. When he met Anya, his desperation climaxed. He offered to squeeze two of the oranges into his mess cup in exchange for a blow job. The time to do both was exactly the same.

"I just picked it up. I watched them myself. It's beautiful thing. They take perfect, round orange spheres like perfect tits and slit them in half."

Marty pauses to lick his lips. A few drops of juice have dried and grown sticky at the corners of his mouth.

"They put each half in silver press. They press fuck out of them. Every single drop. Not drop left. Then, they pour liquid into cup. What you want? I can't get fresher than cup unless I bring you fucking tree."

Anya laughs, but it's joyless. She knows that every Russian longs to visit Florida so they can pick oranges from a tree.

"Yours took ten oranges, cost me $8. I got you large. I got me small." He winks, "That's because you deserve more than me."

The sip makes her gag. "I can't drink it."

"You don't like nothing, Anya. You don't like nothing I bring you anymore. Remember?" Marty sinks lower into the seat, wriggling to make it accommodate his bulk. He strokes his trimmed reddish beard with his hand and combs back the wisps of stray hairs with his fingers. He reminisces.

"Remember what I used to bring? Anything you ask for anytime of day. I run all over town. Didn't matter what town, I run to get it. I didn't never put on tab. You remember when it was cold in Baltimore? Never been so fucking cold in history of temperature, I found hot pastrami."

Anya puts the lid back on the cup of orange juice and returns it to Marty.

"The fucking heat was turned off in the room, cock-sucker," Anya says. "And you, stubborn as a rock, would not change rooms. You think the pastrami kept me from freezing to death? Either I had to crawl into bed next to your slab of fat or die." She makes a sound of repulsion.

Marty smiles with parental tenderness. His upper gums show when he expresses extreme happiness. He loves to hear Anya talk, foul or otherwise. If she calls him "cock-sucker," it doesn't matter. It's good therapy for her to call him foul names. It's good for her to express herself. Like everybody else, she's got frustrations too.

He watches her dress. Her back is nearly unmarred. Her buttocks are young, firm, voluptuous, and untouched by her lack of appetite. They are perfectly accented by two large tufted dimples and a sprig of blond, downy hair. She pulls on a tiny turquoise-colored thong and over its bit of nothing, a pair of tight jeans. She looks at her nails with disgust. "I need polish. When you go out, I need lilac polish."

"We got little problem," Marty glances at the dark window. The bright winter Southern California sun is less than a half-inch away. He checks his watch. It's nearly noon. "There was hang-up."

"Fuck," Anya exhales with exasperation.

"No *problema* because we ain't go far, only six hours, straight road all way."

Marty motions at Anya to come to him. She saunters across the tightly woven carpet. There's a track of round, brown stains beneath her.

"I didn't do that," she points down.

"We leaving anyways."

"Your friend messed up the rug."

"Can you live with it for few more hours?" Marty pulls her forward into his lap. "We going to leave here. We going on drive. You going sleep. Then when we get where we going, it's just few more days." Marty growls affectionately. "And presto."

Anya presses her lower lip with her teeth. She can't smile because it's not yet true. When it's true, then she'll smile. Then, she'll look deeply into his cock-sucker eyes and tell him "fuck off" for the last time.

5

ucking is preferable to lap-dancing. With fucking, you can roll over and close your eyes. With fucking, you're alone with the client. Maybe he makes a lot of noise. Maybe he smells bad. Maybe he wants to talk. These variables degrade a bad experience into something worse, but at least they're brief. Even if he has signed on to spend the night, it's likely he'll sleep. Unless he's got problems and can't come. Or problems and can't get hard. Problems or not, odds are good. Eventually, he'll get bored or tired. Eventually, Anya will be left alone.

With fucking, usually no one is monitoring. Of course, management has peep holes, cameras, two-way mirrors where they can observe. They say that's *within reason*. They want to make sure you haven't jumped out the window. Or told a story about being kept against your will. After you have a bit of seniority, they mostly leave you alone.

Lap-dancing is a group thing. It's a social experience. A party. There are more opportunities to make friends with other girls. But with lap-dancing there is constant supervision. Management snoops around and checks you out. They give you pointers like you're wiggling your ass too much. Or you're not wiggling it enough. You're jiggling your tits too low. Or too high. You're shoving your ass too far in his crotch. Or not far enough. Those sorts of pointers.

They're also very particular about time. They want the clients aroused and thirsty. They want them throwing money around. But they don't want you to waste your time. You can't waste your time. After six minutes, more or less, if the client isn't hard or isn't drinking, it's time to move on. With the promise, of course, that you'll be back soon.

Six minutes is ideal. It's like boiling an egg. You have to get very familiar with time because they don't let you wear a watch. You have to feel the minutes tick inside your head.

Because of the ratio of girls to men, most clients either cling to the bar or sit at tables. They like to sit, look, and wait their turn. Some only want to look. The more who look, the easier your work, but you still get credit for the whole hour.

If management doesn't like your performance, they take you out in front of everyone. They slap you around if they want to make an example. They want to insure the clients are pleased at all times. They want them to see it's a clean, well-run establishment with standards. Slackers aren't tolerated. Everybody pulls their weight. That's how clientele and reputations are established. That's how everyone makes money.

There are two things Anya hates about lap-dancing. First, it requires constant attention. Even if the client is drunk, he wants to watch you, and he wants to know you're watching him. That alone demands incredible stamina. It's exhausting. You can't lie around and use your hand or mouth or cunt. You've got to throw yourself into it. Every limb has to keep moving.

That's why lap-dancers get breaks. Or else you'd collapse from dehydration. Regular breaks are the greatest advantage to lap-dancing.

The second nuisance is the music. Both volume and selection. Theoretically, the musical selection corresponds to the taste of the clientele. Bad pop tuned to the highest decibel. There is one single idiotic mood, constant and unvaried. Party! Party! Party!

Usually, you last a year in the lap-dancing circuit. It's management's way of keeping you tired as well as trained. It's like being a pony. Once you're broken, they move you into more lucrative endeavors.

Practically speaking, it's better to fuck. You get more credits. Lap-dancing is only one dollar per minute. That means no matter how long you wiggle or how much the client spends, you won't make more than $60 in credit per hour.

Fucking costs a client more. With fucking, the average is $150 an hour but you can get up to $300 if you're a little talented.

Anya is excellent at sucking. In addition to beautiful technique, she is also endowed with unusual features. She can turn her tongue completely over. She can curl it like a petal. Or contract it like a cobra's head. She can make it hard like a clit. She can isolate the tip into something tiny enough to enter the hole of a dick. Anya's sucking is in demand. For sucking alone, she sometimes earns an extra $50 credit.

Anya has been fucked in nearly every hole. Holes are an average night's work. Not to mention rubs and drubs between her tits so they can spray her face with cum. That doesn't bother her. Ass-fucking doesn't bother her. Even the ear. If someone wants to hump her ear or eyelids, that's all right too but she doesn't like them to come in her eyes or ears. She's afraid that might give her an infection.

One-on-one is encouraged. Management dislikes a client having more than one girl at a time. It can lead to intimacy between the girls. Or conspiracy and escape. If a client insists on two or more girls at a time, they are carefully watched.

Some clients pay a lot to get rough. Anya is used to it. If they whip her, she knows how to relax into the pain. If they strap her down, she pretends to struggle. If they gag her, she usually doesn't throw up. If they strangle her, she knows a pressure point between their thumb and forefinger that stops them if it hurts.

Management doesn't let them get too rough. For too rough, Anya has a button she can push. Too rough, they get kicked out. No refunds.

Anya does not like foot jobs. Her feet are strong, but she lacks true prehensile abilities. It is hard for her to grab, hold, and massage with her feet. She's clumsy at it, but there are others who are very good. Their toes are long, and they have a particularly strong grip. It's a refined practice reserved for clients with such interests.

Anya does not do nose jobs. That's the most expensive specialty of the house. Anya's nostrils are too small. Men with undersized dicks always want to stick them up a woman's nose. They ask for a gorilla girl to comply. They ask for special girls from Africa who can take it up the nose. A year back, one of the girls died when the cum shot into her brain.

None of the girls knew it, but Marty told Anya she'd had a stroke. He was upset. He needed someone to talk to.

At first, the client thought it was a joke. He thought it was part of the specialty. When he realized she was really dead, he thought management would call the police. He panicked. He was an officer in the system, so naturally he offered to do whatever he could to help.

Management said it wasn't a problem as long as he took the body with him when he left the premises. That's the policy, and it seems *within reason*. After all, if they promise not to notify the authorities, then it's the client's responsibility to dispose of the corpse.

Anya is a pro but never call her a whore. That's a nasty, emotional word. Its usage is discouraged. She's a sex-worker. That's her job title. It implies earnings. It carries benefits. For a professional, there's no emotional resonance. It's business.

6

For Anya, management means Marty and his friends. The friends vary, but Marty is a constant. Marty is head of the management team. He keeps the books. He checks the records. He makes the reports. He processes customer complaints. He orders clothes. He makes recommendations and transport arrangements. He has a half-dozen girls he supervises, but he bears a soft spot for Anya because their grandmothers both came from Moldova. He doesn't understand why her abuse comforts him. Maybe he thinks he deserves it.

It is after ten when Marty gets back to the room. Anya has been waiting impatiently. For the first time in weeks, she is hungry.

"You got something to eat?" Anya asks before Marty even opens the door.

Marty carries a bag with a cold hamburger and fries.

"I told you, I ain't eating junk no more."

"Liberty," Marty remarks sorrowfully.

Inadvertently, Anya repeats the syllables and immediately regrets it. The sound makes a hole in her mouth. She is superstitious. She believes words have power. She believes if you say certain words too much, their power disappears. What they represent disappears.

Marty drops the waxed bag in the trash can. "We can stop on way out of town and buy you carrot. You ready?"

Anya kicks the valise in his direction and puts on her raincoat. "I get so sick of moving around, you know?"

Anya looks despondently at the room. The queen-size bed, rumpled and unmade. The two bedside tables stacked with magazines and a clock radio. The plywood chest of drawers with a phony burl veneer. The dark rectangular windows hung with Venetian blinds and floral drapes. The fussy, uncomfortable loveseat. The square table surrounded by four chairs as if guests were expected. The textured sheet-rock walls painted beige. The sound-proof ceiling. The large television set.

"Why should I bother to complain?" she shrugs. "As soon as we get to the new place, it will look exactly the same."

Marty grunts as he picks up the valise. "Every time you move, I got to move too. And it's not only you. I got to keep track all of you."

"Where's Cerise?" Anya asks.

Cerise is Anya's closest friend. Her name used to be Mary. When she arrived, they gave her the name Cerise. They don't allow Mary or any of its variations: Marian, Miriam, Maryann, Maria, Marie. It's their policy. They say nobody wants to be reminded of religion if they're fucking a young girl who isn't their wife. That's why they changed Mary's name to Cerise.

Cerise likes the new name. It means "cherry" in French. However, if there's a religious client with special needs, someone who insists on having a girl named Mary, they give him Cerise. She even looks like a Mary.

"Upstairs working. Everybody is upstairs."

"I need to see her before I go," Anya demands.

"What you think?" Marty plunks the valise down by the door. "It's too late. She got somebody with her now."

Anya pouts. She hates leaving without good-bye. It's desertion.

"We got to go." Marty stops in the doorway.

"Can't you check her schedule? Can't you do one favor for me?"

"All I fucking do is favors for you. You ever notice that? I bring you orange juice. You know how many people in whole world never taste real oranges in whole fucking life?" Marty holds up a hand and flaps his fingers to indicate millions and millions. He adds, "All they got to drink is dirty water. But you, Anya, you spit it up."

Anya is silent to suggest penitence.

"Didn't I thank you for the orange juice?"

"You thanked me, but you didn't drink it. I should have brought it to Cerise."

"I can't go without her knowing it. Cerise depends on me."

"It's going to make her stronger person, Anya. Believe me, I see it all time. Girls coming, girls leaving. I understand. I had to leave best friend, Igor. I left him in Russia to die. How does that make me feel?" Marty blinks his moist bovine eyes in Anya's direction.

"Are you going to promise me to be good to her?" Anya can feel herself about to cry. It's a nearly unfamiliar sensation.

Marty makes a sign of the cross. "I'm good to everyone. That's my job."

At first, Cerise was a difficult case. She was resistant. But Anya took Cerise under her wing. She convinced her there was no gain in resistance. Anya was well-rewarded for her ability at persuasion. Now she loves Cerise and feels responsible.

Cerise is quiet, beautiful, and very young. She's white. Not sickly white from life indoors but translucent like quartz. Her veins show through her skin all over her body. She has long black, board-straight hair, black eyes, and her face is composed and serene. She's from Romania. She was raised in an orphanage. Her parents were executed. She doesn't know why. She went to the orphanage when she was ten. Now she's seventeen. When she came, she was a virgin. They like to call her the Sepulcher.

"You coming?"

Marty takes a step and yanks Anya's arm. If she refuses to do anything, she gets fined. Sometimes they fine you as much as $5,000.

"I can't leave yet," Anya sighs as she slinks back onto the loveseat. Maybe she should refuse to go on special assignment. Maybe she should risk the fine. Maybe she should plan to stay one more year. Then, she would be able to take care of Cerise.

Marty takes two steps into the room and delivers a sharp punch exactly at Anya's temple. She crumples to the floor. Her eyelids flutter, and a bubble of spit forms on her lower lip.

He picks her up in his arms and kicks the valise towards the door. When he exits the building, he hears a weird noise at the corner of the street. He peers at the telephone wire and limbs of a jacaranda tree. He can't tell where it's coming from but wishes the fuck it would stop.

7

I-5 is a paved, divided four-lane highway that bifurcates the Central Valley of California. It follows no river, track, trail, or ancient pathway. Its route is entirely its own. Its logic, the logic of efficiency. There are hills but no curves. The road is straight like a surgical incision.

At its southern end, I-5 traverses the city of Los Angeles, intersects the Pacific coast at San Clemente, and terminates at the Mexican border in Tijuana. However, the true definition of I-5 is the scar of road that commences north of Los Angeles at the base of the Grapevine – the long, winding, elevated marvel through the Tehachapi Mountains – and extends almost a thousand miles through the length of central California, Oregon, and Washington over the Canadian border to Vancouver.

This is the quickest driving route between the north and southern parts of the West Coast, averaging 20,000 vehicles per day. The two highest passes are Tejon (4,183 feet) coming out of Los Angeles and Black Butte Summit (3,899 feet) in Siskiyou County. Cars typically travel ninety miles an hour, slowing only when numerous trucks crowd the highway.

Accidents are few unless there is tule fog. Tule fog is the dense impenetrable winter fog that emanates from the ground like miasma. It's impossible to see more than a few inches in tule fog. It hangs in the air like a fold of vaporous drapery, encasing the road. If you speed into it, you easily crash into the back of other stunned motorists.

Tules themselves are the bulrushes once harvested by native California tribes (Ohlone, Miwok, Yokut, Patwin, Maidu, Kardow) and used to make clothing, mats, rafts, roofs, cradles, and baskets. The natives are mostly gone, and their techniques of basketry all but vanished, but the tule remain.

Along California's Central Valley are the mega-farms and mega-orchards that feed the entire country. Years ago its natural weather pattern – rain in winter, drought in summer – was altered through a complex system of dams and aqueducts. Now from May through October, billions of gallons of water are pumped every year into the extremely hot, otherwise dry fields.

Voracious cattle ranches vie with farmers for land and water along I-5. Halfway between Los Angeles and Sacramento is the immense Harris Ranch adjacent to the road with its 100,000 head of beef cattle. The stench alerts even the most oblivious driver of the filth and offal that constitute domesticated animal life on an imperial scale. Every day the Central Valley's beef and dairy ranches produce millions of gallons of liquid manure that in turn toxify the air with methane, hydrogen sulfide, and ammonia gases.

The newest roadside attractions on I-5 are California prisons. Penal institutions have been constructed on empty desolate stretches of non-arable land to house the ever-growing population of the state's criminals: over 170,000, mostly men, mostly black and Latino, and mostly incarcerated for nonviolent crimes. Prisons now insure the economic viability of small Central Valley towns where the increasing automation in agriculture offers fewer jobs for the young and uneducated.

When the first stretches of I-5 opened north of Los Angeles, there was nothing. No gas, no food, no lodging. Now oases of fast-food franchises and motels frequently pop up. However, once you are on I-5, it is difficult to leave. It's a mesmerizing drive for hundreds of miles, straight and unveering.

∽

It is past midnight. Marty's minivan has completed the wide, looping, symphonic curves of the Grapevine and begun the four-hundred mile ride north. His assistant, Pedro, is driving. A small, hirsute, wiry man, Pedro looks like a tarantula wrapped around the steering wheel.

Marty dozes in the front seat, his head contentedly collapsed back on his neck while his mouth opens every time he snores. Marty is a man who can sleep anywhere.

Anya is curled around a pillow clutched against her chest. She wakes with a shiver, for it is winter and cold in the Central Valley.

At the rear of the van, a bench for extra passengers has been locked into place. A girl lies across it. Anya doesn't recognize her. Anya doesn't know how the girl got in the van or remember how she herself got in. The girl is tiny under a blanket. She doesn't stir. Anya can't even hear her breathe. Maybe she's a corpse Marty plans to dump.

"Fuck," Anya says groggily.

"Yeah?" Pedro answers as if that's his name. It's the English word that is most familiar.

"Stop! Fuck!" Anya cries out.

"Canno-stop," Pedro replies calmly.

"Marty," Anya wails. "Make him stop."

With a start, Marty falls forward in his seat and hits his head on the windshield. The girl in the rear of the van doesn't move.

"Can't you drive?" He seethes at Pedro. "You bump around like fucking ball."

"I got to pee," Anya groans.

Marty pivots his head to the back as if he hasn't understood.

"Nostash-un," Pedro says.

"Marty, tell him to fucking speak English, then tell him to fucking stop."

Marty grabs the wheel and swerves the car to the shoulder of the road.

"Get out, make it quick," he orders roughly. His head hurts, and they're already behind schedule.

Marty prides himself on punctuality. He faults their delay on Anya's new diet and Pedro's inability to read road signs. It's the pain of always having to deal with immigrants. That's his major complaint. The Mexicans who work for the organization are illiterate, at least in English. The girls are spoiled, especially the Russians who take advantage of him. That's why he has to hit them sometimes. He doesn't like to hit them, but some of them act like Romanovs. It's not his fault when they're late, but it is his responsibility. He's hopeful no one at the other end cares.

Barefoot, Anya staggers out of the car, unzips her jeans, squats at the side of the road. There is little traffic, but one trucker cannot help but honk. It's a frightening blast of sound across the otherwise cold, silent, empty fields. Anya waves her middle finger his way and prays that he and his ugly rig tumble off a cliff.

Marty pulls out his gun. Now for certain, he has a headache.

Pedro sits in the car. His body is stationary as he faces north, the direction they must drive for at least four more hours until they turn and head west towards Oakland.

Pedro places his head in his hands. He shuts his eyes so he won't be tempted to look at the beautiful Anya's naked ass.

"It's fucking cold, Marty. Where's my coat?"

Marty reaches into a canvas duffle on the floor of the van and lifts out two coats. Anya's is a black pea-coat with white fake fur lining, collar, and cuffs. She feels it makes her look aristocratic. That pleases her. Two years ago, Marty found it in a catalog and ordered it for her. It was more expensive than the other coats, but she said it didn't matter. It went on her tab. Out of thousands, what did $250 matter?

"I'm sorry I hit you," Marty says.

Anya shivers. She buttons up her coat, turns up the collar, and searches in the pockets for a pair of white angora gloves. "Doesn't the heater work?"

"Don't you listen what I'm telling you anymore, Anya? We had to go and you know." Marty's voice trails off. "I said I was sorry."

"I hear you. But what you want me to say? You fucking irritate me when you apologize. You want me to say you ain't a cock-sucker?"

Marty looks at the spaceship dashboard. "Pedro, how fucking heater works in car?"

Pedro mumbles, "Heeter bye-bye."

"Where's heater?"

"*Descompuesto*," Pedro adds.

"Either speak English or I throw you out car." Marty points to the side of the road and yells, "You see out there? There's nothing out there. There's nothing and nobody. You want to walk home from there?"

Pedro shakes his head obediently. His hairy spider fingers tighten over the steering wheel. It's a bad job, he thinks. The only good thing is once in a while he gets to see someone's beautiful titties and beautiful ass.

"So you were saying?" Marty inquires as if they were suddenly inside a drawing room.

"Brow-kin," Pedro tries.

"As in bro-ken?"

The driver nods.

"Heater broken been determined," Marty conveys to Anya.

"It only took fifteen minutes. Why don't you hire somebody with a brain?"

Marty smiles broadly. His upper gums show when he is pleased. The gums are soft, pale gray, and inflamed. They look like scallops.

"You got to pay someone with brain. This guy, we don't pay much. Sometimes he gets little bread, a few little peeks now and then. He gets place to stay, some food to eat. When we found him, he didn't have papers, money, nothing. Some dirty clothes on dirty back. He didn't have toilet even to shit in. It makes person loyal after you find somebody like that."

"He's ugly," Anya sighs. She has seen many ugly men. Handsome men don't seem to find their way to her unless they have problems. If they're handsome, then maybe they want to pee on her stomach or face. Or slap her for kicks. When they finish, guys like that aren't handsome anymore.

"He's hairy fucker. He got hairs coming out ears. You notice that? If he climbs on you, you think fuzzy spider landed."

"Shut up," Anya says.

"You know what we like best about Pedro?" Marty chuckles and tugs on Anya's sleeve. "He don't complain."

8

Inside the black night there are planets, distant and near, aggregates of colored lights flashing on the horizon. They rise in the blackness and recede as the van passes by. Inside their orbit are the giant neon signs with the familiar colors and familiar brands. Planet gas stations, planet restaurants and motels. There are no surprises. From exit to exit they are the same. Or in between are the exits with no reason to stop. NO SERVICES say the signs. Anya feels badly for these exits. Orphan exits. NO SERVICES is a cipher, a void. Hopeless places where no one goes.

Another twenty miles pass. A truck stop flashes: DIESEL OPEN 24. Another twenty miles pass. Marty grumbles to Pedro. Anya can't hear what they say. They whisper in the front seat. Their voices rub up against each other like insect wings. Russian hairy and Mexican hairy, they both disgust her.

They are stopping. That's a surprise. Usually, they don't stop for hours. Maybe if there's a toilet emergency, but the emergency has already come and gone.

They exit I-5 and travel up a ramp.

"We're stopping?" Anya asks.

Marty grumbles again to Pedro. He's in a bad mood. They're late, and now this little detour will make them later.

Anya eyes the Denny's sign, the planter boxes, the double glass doors, and the customers with bent heads eating and sipping coffee in booths along the window. She likes the Belgian Waffle Platter and hash browns.

"Can I get breakfast?" she asks.

"Maybe," Marty says. "If we have to wait, maybe."

"Wait on what?" She wants to know.

"You give me headaches with questions."

Pedro drives slowly by Denny's. He makes the first left, turns around, and enters their parking lot. There are three cars, one pick-up truck.

Anya bites a cuticle. "It's out of the ordinary, isn't it?"

Marty is not interested in a discussion.

He opens the van door, looks up to the vast black sky only slightly diluted by neon. He spies the Great Bear, the sign of Russia Motherland. He touches the part of his shirt over his heart. His family, he sighs. They believed he would study engineering. They believed he came to America to go to school. Once a month he too writes letters home.

He inspects the shiny red truck parked in the Denny's lot, the clean mud flaps, the double cab, the leather seats, and the empty, spotless bed. Instead of a license plate, there is an ad from Three-Way Chevrolet, 3800 California Avenue, Bakersfield. Marty reads the phone number too as if that's a clue.

"Clue or test?" Marty likes to say.

"Okay, out," he shouts.

Anya makes a move.

"Not you," he barks.

"But I'm hungry."

Marty commands. "Shake her, then breakfast."

For a second Anya doesn't know what he means. She leans over the seat divider and touches the body under the blanket. She has never touched a corpse except her Baba's face at the funeral.

The girl lifts her head. It's tiny. Her eyelashes bat like a sleepy child.

"Okay, Lily. You're here."

Lily doesn't move.

"Tell her to get up," Marty says.

"Get up," Anya says softly.

She lifts her feet slowly off the seat. Anya can see she's barefoot.

Her feet are tiny, brown. Her unpainted toenails look like seashells. She has on bell-bottom jeans, a small pink t-shirt, and a pink cardigan sweater. The outfit of a kindergartner.

Marty opens the hatch door of the van. "You're here," he announces.

The girl looks around. There is nothing to see except a few commercial businesses along the side of a concrete road.

"Does she understand English?" Anya asks.

"How fuck should I know?" Marty doesn't like this little job. It's a favor he didn't want to do. Even he has scruples. Even he draws the line.

"Do you speak English?" Anya asks, touching the soft, babyish hand.

The girl's mouth makes no movement. It looks as if it has never spoken.

"Tell Lily this where she going," Marty directs Anya.

"Is she deaf too?"

"Just do it."

"But she can hear you," Anya complains, then complies. "This is where you're going."

Pedro waits in the car while Anya follows Marty and the girl into the restaurant. Two men from a back booth wave at them. They slide over to make room.

The men look related, brothers or cousins. One is cross-eyed, the other bald. They've already eaten breakfast. The bald one pushes his plate in front of Lily. She doesn't open her mouth to eat either.

Anya looks at the men. They're expensively dressed in cashmere sweaters. Nice cologne. They're forty, she surmises. She can't imagine what they do in the middle of nowhere. SERVICES and NO SER-VICES equally depress her, except for the temptation of a Belgian Waffle Platter.

She nibbles at a biscuit on the table.

"Help yourself," the man's voice is so loud she jumps.

"Her too?" the other one asks.

"No," Marty says brusquely. Underneath the table one fist socks another. He is opening and closing his hands, thinking he can't afford to slug these American ranchers. There would be consequences.

"What's her name?"

"Lily like flower your mother put in vase at Easter."

"Lily," the man's voice booms. "I'm Pete," he extends his hand. "This is my brother, Clem."

Lily does nothing. She doesn't look or speak. Pete picks up her hand like a twig.

"Does she speak English?" He asks.

"How fuck should I know?" Marty says.

"Hey," Clem grabs the check. "We don't need that."

"What's she?" Pete asks him, nodding to Anya.

"Russian like me."

"Pretty," Pete says winking at Anya. "I like her."

"Like all you want," Marty shrugs and orders a cup of coffee. "You didn't ask for Russian. You ask for Thai. Lily Thai."

"I can see that," Pete smiles, trying to be friendly. "She looks like a little eggroll. You got girls from everywhere?"

"I don't got girls," Marty insists. "This girl my cousin and this other Lily girl your friend who friend of boss ask me to pick up in front of warehouse downtown. That all I do."

"I want something," Anya whispers.

"What you want, pretty?" the bald rancher asks.

Marty signals the waitress. "Hash brown go," he says. "Three order."

"One two three orders of hash browns?" the waitress repeats to make sure.

"No," Marty says, "one two three four five, put with ketchup."

"Come on," Clem says. "Get the girl."

The two ranchers rise. "Lily." It's Pete's loud voice. "We're going now," he explains.

Lily doesn't move. Her eyes search out Anya.

Anya stares at the biscuit. Beside it is an open plastic container of strawberry preserves. Strawberries remind her of Ba, the blue china saucer delivered magically to her bed. She doesn't look up from the biscuit and jam as the girl is pushed out of the booth.

"Lily," the man's voice has lowered. He whistles to her like a small animal.

Maybe she's mute, Anya thinks. Anya doesn't want to see. She shuts her eyes and silently calls, *Ba, Ba, Ba.*

9

"You want sleep?" Marty pulls a cylinder from his shirt pocket. He shakes a couple of white glossy pills onto his palm. "You should sleep."

Anya looks at the empty, black ground on both sides of the road. "I don't think I can miss this," she says contemptuously.

He replaces the pills, tightens the cap, and wipes his hands on his coat.

The night has grown overcast, but the crescent of a luminous quarter moon is occasionally clear. On the far right side of the road are faint outlines of mountains.

"Where fuck is this?"

A coyote howls in reply.

Marty reads the sign. "Seventeen miles to Lost Hills."

Anya muses. "It's a good name, but where are the hills?"

Marty points to the dim, jagged shapes in the distance. He looks at the map.

Anya's skeptical eye returns to the landscape. Its loneliness suits her. She wants desperately to be alone. If they offered to stop the van, she would get out and take her chances in Lost Hills.

But they won't stop. They won't offer. They will drive until they reach their destination. And only Marty knows her destination. That is the grossest humiliation of all. Even more humiliating than fucking ugly men. Only they know where she is going, and it's a secret. She has no idea.

Anya stares at the night. Thoughts of a future tumble around. She is dreaming of liberty. It's a dream where she unlocks a door from the inside and walks into daylight. The sun is gleaming. Everything – the streets, buildings, people who pass by – gleams from the brightness of the sun. Sun-worshipers, she dreams. Outside a man is waiting. He is not a filthy Russian, German, American, or Japanese. He is not ugly, hairy, and fat. He's a United States astronaut. Young, small, well-built, and lithe. Because most of his face is covered with a space mask, only his eyes are visible. His eyes are as soft and brown as a deer. There is nothing hard inside them. He tells her that from outer space, he has listened to her private thoughts. Now he has returned to Earth, at this very moment of liberation, to meet her. He has heard her thoughts and knows her innermost self. He regards her as if she's innocent. All her humiliations crumble. They fall like a wall. She is innocent, and now she is free. Her whole body trembles with this claim of selfhood.

She is dreaming in English. Her English is good enough to come to her in dreams. It's the English of television. She guesses that of her four years in the States, at least one year – and by that, she means over 8,000 hours – has passed watching television. She watches in the day or very late at night. The soaps, of course, are favorites. The characters, like her, mostly live indoors. When they go out, she gets to go out with them. If the news is on, she mutes the sound. She only wants to look at pictures. She wants to look at sports played outdoors in fresh air. She especially likes golf. She likes the nature shows if they're about fishes or birds, but the large mammals scare her. She likes old movies late at night where the outdoors looks even more real in black-and-white.

The astronaut takes her by the hand. She leans into his shoulder because he is good. And now she is good too. His forgiveness makes her good.

Between Anya's ears a loud, phrenetic combination of horns and guitar explodes. She is awake like a cat, alert and predatory. From behind she grabs Pedro's neck and squeezes the hairy, unshaved stalk.

"Turn the fucking music off," she commands.

Pedro squirms out of her grip and looks helplessly to Marty.

"I told him he could listen." Marty yawns loudly. "He's sleepy. He needs something pep him up."

"Then give him a magic pill."

Marty searches his pocket for another vial of pills, also small and white with tiny crosses engraved on one side. He hands a pill to Pedro who obediently swallows. Marty swallows too and offers a couple to Anya. She grabs them and puts them in her pocket. She saves pills like coupons. She can trade them for alcohol.

Anya slips back down on the seat and pulls her coat closer around her neck. She can faintly smell the girl. She never saw a Thai girl before, Thai or Indian. A few Chinese, a few Africans, a few Filipinos, but mostly she knows Russians, Ukrainians, Moldovans, Romanians.

"Cultural diversity," she has heard on television. She is not sure what it means.

Sometimes Marty says it as a joke. When she asked him once to explain, he said, "It's term that make men think they understanding world." He pointed to his crotch, "No difference."

"Any vodka?" Anya meekly asks.

"Oh, I forgot," he apologizes gleefully. "I should have remembered to pick up the Stoly. Anya, you're such a lush."

She reddens. She'd rather be called a whore than a drunk.

"It helps me sleep," she protests indignantly.

"It makes you ugly," he retorts. "Remember how ugly it made your mother?"

"Shut up. You never met my mother."

Marty laughs maliciously, "I don't need to meet her."

"Shut up, you son-of-a-pig," Anya cries.

"Today you love your mother?"

"Pig," Anya elongates the single syllable.

Marty's lips rise above his gums. He's pleased that he has aroused her.

"I only meant," he says, "that without your mother, you not here."

Anya closes her eyes. It's true, what he says, but she is unsure if that is bad or good.

10

One minute there is a murky but visible night, and the next the van has passed through a gaseous wall and entered a spectral fortress.

Pedro slams the brakes and curses in Spanish. Marty's head cracks the windshield. Anya rolls to the floor of the backseat. The van slides onto the shoulder of road and stops.

"Fuck," Marty feels for the gash in his forehead.

The van is enveloped with a veil of tule fog. The disembodied head-lights going south and taillights heading north twinkle in diffused red and white orbs. The cars are ghost ships painfully inching through a foggy sea towards harbor. Slowly, they pass by. Slowly, they move on. No one stops. No one sees. In an instant, the fog has swallowed any sign of mishap.

"Dumb-fuck Mexican," Marty screams, jamming his shirttail against his head.

For a moment, Pedro's mind is still, but his body has begun to jerk around. He opens his door. He gets out. He runs around the van. He kicks the tires. He checks for dents. When he re-enters the vehicle, he shouts victoriously, *"No problema!"*

"No problema," Marty repeats viciously in a thick Russian accent. "Except middle of fucking cloud." He is sick to his stomach. He can smell the sticky blood. His shirt has soaked through. He reaches for a rag under the seat. "I'm going bleed to death here in cloud," he laments.

Marty pats his head. The blood makes him gag. He opens the door and pukes into the barely visible grass.

"What is this?" He holds his hand out, arm's length. His fingertips are invisible.

Anya trembles with fright. It was nearly a tragedy, she thinks: to die in a fog and never be a sun-worshiper.

"Anya, you hear me?" Marty yells.

"I can," she whispers. She sounds faint. Her breath is white like mist.

"What you think it is?"

"Poison," Anya says. Everything that touches her is poison, the opposite of the sun. It isn't clear or bright but opaque, ominous. "Leave him. I can drive."

"You talk crazy now." Marty protests. "If you get stopped, we fucked worse than fucked right now."

11

A bright, curious child is a calculating child. She schemes to get what she wants. She tries one tactic and gets spanked. She tries another and goes without dinner. She tries a third and a hairy paw puts its fingers between her plump, little legs. The punishments surprise her in their harshness, their insult, their humiliation. She becomes more cunning. She comes to a turning point, a crossroads, a milestone: either she must suppress her curiosity or commit herself to trouble.

Calculation has long been gone from Anya's scope. It disappeared several weeks after she arrived in the States. It was fucked out of her, so to speak. Recently however, she has been thinking of the future. The future now extends far beyond a set of locked doors. A dim confusion of anxieties and desires have begun to reformulate. She feels a lively cunning, an awakening to life.

The tule fog thickens. Five feet from the van Pedro vanishes. He believes it's safer to walk than drive. He has gone by foot to look for an exit off the highway.

Marty stretches out on the backseat, stanching his wounded head with a towel. He is weak and in shock. His nerves are jangled from the combination of amphetamines and the blow on his head. The wound has begun to throb. His nausea is constant.

Anya analyzes the situation. The van is intact and the keys within reach. The locked attaché case with cash and identity papers is in the rear compartment. She calculates her chances. In the short run, they are promising. Then, she remembers the great lesson of her childhood: short-run calculations are usually fucked.

Marty pukes on the floor of the van. His beard is now scarlet with blood.

Anya moves into the driver's seat and turns over the ignition. The car starts easily, perfectly. She drives forward. No problem. She jams the gear stick in reverse. No problem. She feels for the brake. She has not driven in over four years, but it's no problem. She knows how to drive.

"What you doing?" A muffled voice calls from the back.

"Yes," Anya simply replies.

She backs the car around on the shoulder. A wheel has never moved so loosely in her hands. At first, the automatic steering frightens her. There's nothing to control. It feels like a noodle, but after a moment she finds the tension.

She moves slowly across the north-bound lanes and heads down a shallow gully that divides the traffic. The lights of oncoming cars lunge out of the fog, but they are above her. All sound is above her too. With the decreased visibility, her hearing has become acute. Somewhere she hears a hairy spider voice crying, "*Socorro! Socorro!*"

Inside the gully she putters along a couple of hundred yards before the tule fog evaporates entirely. The gully levels out. Anya positions the gear-stick to 1, pushes the accelerator to the floor, and reaches the top of the short incline. The van quickly slips into the scant stream of south-bound traffic.

At the first possible exit, Anya leaves the highway. Near the access road is an entrance to one of California's newer prisons, renamed "correctional facility." Tall cyclone fences crowned by rolls of razor wire surround a dark, dusty field and an indeterminate number of low, dark buildings. The field is empty except for look-out towers at the corners. Each thirty-foot hexagonal tower has a glass box and air conditioning unit on top. A searchlight from one tower lazily sweeps across the area.

Anya reads the words: CORRECTIONAL FACILITY. Even a foreigner can perceive the joke.

Anya pulls up to a long one-storey concrete building, freshly painted a soft green, the color of moss. Facing the building is a crescent-shaped lawn with a flagpole in its center. When Anya sees the bear on the state flag, like Marty she is reminded of Russia. But she harbors no love for her country. She believes it was her country that ruined her.

In front of the building, wooden posts form a portico or outdoor waiting area. There's a carved wooden sign – Visitors Center – over the front door, and several terra cotta pots with large cactuses stand by the entryway.

Anya leaves the engine running as she enters the glass doors.

The guard rises and straightens his jacket. He turns down the radio. He looks directly at Anya and nods professionally. He notices she has no eyebrows. He also sees there is blood on her neck and hands.

The guard is unprepared for emergencies. During his six months on the job, there has been nothing to do. Visiting hours on weekends and holidays have gone smoothly. Trucks entering and exiting the facility on weekdays have gone smoothly. In fact, when he interviewed for the position, he was told there would be almost nothing to do. They asked if he had the capacity to do nothing for eight hours. Although he reassured them, they hesitated to hire him because he looked energetic. He looked too eager, too bright. They tried to dissuade him. They said it was no job for a man with ambition. Finally, when they made their offer, they recommended he refuse it. Later, he was told it was part of the test.

The youth did not tell them he had no choice. He feared it would sound ungrateful. Or unpatriotic. Instead, he humbly thanked them. They issued him uniforms at once and apologized that there wasn't time for official training. He had to begin immediately. Later, they promised, he would receive training. Eventually, he would learn to use firearms and emergency riot tactics. So far, he has only learned to sleep standing up.

"May I help you?" he asks courteously. In short, practiced phrases, his accent disappears.

Anya regards his square, brown face. It's not ugly, but it is closed like a stone.

"We need a hospital." She mirrors his stoniness.

"This is not a hospital."

Anya nods with fatigue and understanding. She looks out at the field and the dark, cheerless buildings. A couple of cottonwoods break the horizon.

"We need a doctor."

"This is not a hospital," the young man repeats. He has not been prepped for off-hour visitors.

"But you have a doctor," Anya insists.

The guard hesitates. He has been instructed never to give out information about the prison facility. Under all circumstances, he should indicate nothing about the staff or resident population. He has been warned about journalists and terrorists. He has pondered why either would interest themselves in this particular facility, but he clearly recognizes that in such matters he is ignorant. And naive. These are matters he doesn't understand. He has overheard his superiors speak of terrorists. Sometimes they speak in hushed, fearful tones. Other times they are loud and boastful, inviting terrorists to mess with them.

"Is there a doctor here?" Anya questions impatiently.

The young man hears an inflection that is not deferential, only barely polite. From appearances, however, he would not take her for a terrorist.

"I am not permitted to give out information." He delivers his instructions, hoping they will prompt her to back up, turn around, and drive away.

"Come," Anya points to the van.

The guard follows her outside into the raw, cold night. She opens the side door so he can see. On the backseat is a blood-sotted shape of a face and a bloody tweed jacket.

Anya whispers, "Marty."

There is a low moan.

The young man's expression is charged with concern. Conscience and protocol draw sides in his weary mind. He rubs his eyes like a boy. Perhaps the apparition of the girl and the ghoul will go away.

"If he dies here, you will be responsible," Anya says, knitting her non-existent eyebrows towards the center of her forehead.

Anya sees she has made an impression.

The guard goes back into the Visitors Center and presses a button. It is the first time he has used it. The abnormally loud buzzer inside the small box startles him.

"It is José, sir," he admits reluctantly.

"Yo José." The intercom amplifies the voice to a shout.

José can hear a television in the background.

"Someone is here," he muffles his voice.

At the other end, the sergeant haws as if he just heard the punchline to a joke. "Someone?"

"I don't know," José says. "I don't know who it is."

"Didja ask?" The sergeant cracks himself up.

José reviews his brief conversation with the woman. So far, he has done nothing irregular. "I didn't ask because there's nobody on the roster scheduled to arrive."

"Fucking A," the sergeant checks his watch. "Business don't start at 3 am. We both fucking know that."

José glances at the van. Anya catches his attention and makes a motion that she wants to come inside.

"Is it a chick?" the sergeant asks.

"Yeah," José cringes.

Once again the sergeant laughs. "She's so horny she had to rush over here. I seen that before. Chicks begging to get in. Chicks who couldn't wait for visiting day. They get that way when their hummer's locked up. Sometimes they let us fuck them. You can probably take care of her yourself, José. She won't even notice if you some kind of beaner."

José hesitates. "They got blood on them. They don't look too good."

The sergeant is suddenly alert. He does not like the combination of strangers and blood in the middle of the night. If there had been an accident, he'd have heard from the CHP. If there had been an accident, somebody on the road would have called 911.

"The blood look real?" He asks.

José regards the tinted windows and open door of the van. He is not sure. He has never seen fake blood.

"I am not totally sure," he confesses guiltily.

"Fuck," the sergeant can only say. He despairs they've put a wet-back on graveyard shift who doesn't know what blood looks like.

12

"Marty," Anya says. "You still alive?"

"Yeah," he grunts. "Where are we?"

"It's okey-dokey," she says. "Okey-dokey" is one of their favorite American expressions they picked up from late night movies.

"Okey-dokey," Marty mumbles. "Where's Pedro?"

Anya doesn't answer. She aches. Her bones ache. She can feel a knot on the back of her head.

Through the glass doors, she looks at the guard in the Visitors Center. He catches her eye and makes a little space between his thumb and forefinger to signify, "Give me another minute."

She starts to smile, but she is blinded by a dense bank of flood-lights that have suddenly been illuminated. Anya shuts her eyes. Then clamps her palms over her ears as a high-pitch, high-alert siren wounds its piercing arc of sound out into the night. It screams for several seconds, stops, and then begins again, as if recovering for the next round of terrifying effort.

Lights in all the buildings have gone on, and the dark empty field is now baldly bright. Several rabbits bounce across the field towards the road.

Coming towards Anya from the right are a dozen sleepy guards, jogging in a V-formation. They have on helmets and heavy-soled boots. The straps of their semi-automatic assault rifles have been slung around their necks and the barrels of the guns rest loosely between their hands. Fifty feet from the van, they stop, point their weapons, and advance slowly.

Anya shrieks.

"Anya, what fuck?" Marty manages to lift his head. He's a bloody horror. Inadvertently, her shrieks have begun to syncopate with the alarm siren.

Each of the guards takes a position at the back, front, and sides of the van. Their aim is level with the tinted windows. As ordered by his superior, José has also drawn a pistol and left his post. He points it at the van's front left tire in case they try to escape.

Marty barks to Anya, "Put hands up."

Quickly, he raises his. The sleeves of his jacket, the flesh on his wrists and fingers are as bloody as his face.

Anya continues to shriek, but now her arms are frantically lifted over her head.

The sergeant cautiously approaches the van. He has lowered his rifle. The woman's shrieks have confused him. He wants her to stop. He is going to ask her nicely, and if she can't stop, he plans to knock her across the face.

Anya stares with white-eyed fright at the helmeted man coming towards her. As he walks, he motions her to be quiet. Although Anya opens her mouth to scream, nothing comes out.

The sergeant sticks his gun through the open side door, pointing it to the floor. Anya can't see his face, only the visor of his helmet blackened by the glare of floodlights.

Anya gasps. It is obvious from the gurgle in her throat that she will soon start screaming again.

The sergeant grabs her and says, "Shut up."

"Shut up, Anya," Marty echoes.

The sergeant waves the gun in the direction of the rear compartment. "How many total?"

"Two," Marty says. The taste of blood in his mouth and his half-upright position have made him sick to his stomach again.

"You and the girl?" He asks.

Marty stretches down on the floor. "We had accident," he murmurs.

The sergeant motions to a subordinate to lift the hatch of the back compartment and check.

"In the fog," Anya adds.

All the guards have lowered their guns. José lifts the flap of his leather holster and replaces his pistol. He is embarrassed by the commotion. He feels it's his fault. He has been ordered to call and have the high-alert alarm system turned off. The hideous sound suddenly stops, and the lights inside the prison buildings are extinguished.

"After the accident, I drove here to find a doctor." Anya says, matter-of-fact and reasonable.

The sergeant hears an accent in her thick open vowels. He points to the sign: CORRECTIONAL FACILITY.

"Can you read that?"

Anya nods. She decides she won't mention her assumption that a prison might have a doctor.

"Just wanna make sure you ain't lost." The sergeant looks around at the guards who have clustered by a potted prickly pear to smoke. "Ain't much of a hospital we got here," he replies. Then, he haws his signature laugh that punctuates almost everything he has to say.

The guards nod and laugh and smoke in response. The smoke helps calm their adrenalin. Soon, they'll be able to get back to sleep.

"Your hubby got hurt?" the sergeant asks.

"Cousin," Anya affirms with a shake of her head.

He winks back at Marty. "I think we can fix you up with some First Aid. Right, boys?"

"Yes, sir," they yell in unison.

"Have to park over in the visitors' lot." He waves at José. "Beaner will show you."

José grins. He is relieved he did not have to shoot his gun.

"We have to see your I.D." The sergeant lists by rote the acceptable items of identification: a valid state drivers' license with a picture that isn't laminated, a valid state Department of Motor Vehicles Identification Card with a picture that isn't laminated, a valid Armed Forces Identification Card with a picture, an Identification Card issued by the United States Department of Justice Immigration and Naturalization Services, a valid passport with a picture, or a picture identification issued by the Mexican Consulate entitled Matricula Consular de Alta

Seguridad (MCAS). He has trouble pronouncing the Spanish words.

Anya starts to panic. She has never been asked for I.D. First, she panics, but then her excitement is followed by cunning. I.D. is freedom. With I.D. she can go anywhere.

Marty reaches into his blood-stained jacket and pulls out two Russian passports: Sergei Shamkin and Nelly Shamkin. It surprises Anya to see her picture inside a passport.

The sergeant looks at it with admiration. It's more attractive than the actual girl.

"You look good," he says.

Anya and Marty say nothing.

"Can he walk?"

Anya looks at Marty. The wound on the forehead has started to stiffen into a ridge of glassy ooze. Smears of tissue-thin burgundy veneer coat his eyes and cheeks. Coagulated rivulets clot his beard.

"I don't think so," Anya says. "He lost too much blood."

"No *problema*," the chief smiles with accommodation. "We got a gurney to take him in. We got wheelchairs too. You don't know how they gonna show up here. Most got legs but you never know." He snaps an order for two guards to run get the gurney. "Got a cripple just two days ago. If I were a cripple," he muses thoughtfully, "I wouldn't wanna be in jail."

13

There is only one problem as the gurney enters the Visitors Center. Marty's gun sets off the alarm. A moment of panic erupts while the sergeant removes and inspects the weapon, admiring the steel-blue sheen and Swiss precision. It's a SIG P210 and cost over $2,000. Marty's boss, Kupkin, gave it to him for his thirtieth birthday.

It ranks among his three most treasured possessions, which include a photograph of his mother on her wedding day and a valuable third edition of Pushkin's *Eugene Onegin*, which appeared in print on the day of his death in 1837. Marty can recite from *Eugene Onegin*, chapter and verse, and cannot utter VI.32 without a stream of tears:

> *Quite still and strangely placid seeming,*
> *He lay in deathly torpor swooned,*
> *His breast pierced through and through, and steaming,*
> *The lifeblood trickled from his wound.*

Marty looks wistfully over at the gun, half-dazed.

"It's a crime to bring onto the grounds: any weapon, firearm, ammunition, explosive device, tear gas, pepper spray, alcohol or controlled substance, cameras and/or recording devices." The sergeant reads from the Visiting Guidelines. "Your cousin got a carry-license with him?"

He stares into Anya's hypnotic eyes. He had not fully noticed them while she was shrieking her head off. Then, his attention had been fixated on the blood-soaked man in the rear of the van. However, now he can barely refrain from staring at her face and form. He considers his taste in women excellent and rates Anya in his top category of "most attractive." She is tall. He likes that. He also likes that she wears stiletto heels to make herself taller. He especially likes her thick thatch of blond hair, prominent breasts, skin-tight jeans, lanky legs, and flirtatious ass. Even her crooked teeth appeal to him. The only thing missing are her eyebrows.

"It's in his attaché case," Anya smiles. She likes saying "attaché" with the flourish of an accent. She took a year of French in school. She believes she has a talent for languages. Her facility with English confirms it. In the future, she plans to work as a translator.

The sergeant quotes again from the Visiting Guidelines on prohibited attire: "Clothing that exposes the breast and chest area, the genital area, or buttocks." He likes enunciating these words. "Sheer or transparent garments, strapless or 'spaghetti' strap tops."

Anya looks down at her low-cut sweater. "But I didn't know," she appeals.

"Usually, we make the girls change out there in the trailer, but since you ain't going inside." The sergeant looks approvingly at Anya. Although he prides himself on good intuition, he is not beyond precaution. Before they leave, he will insist on inspecting the gun license.

They move Marty into a meeting room at the back of the Visitors Center. There's a microwave and small refrigerator, metal tables and a dozen metal chairs. A row of windows looks directly into the prison grounds.

Most of the guards have completed First Aid courses. It's required. One even went to a year of nursing school. He commences to clean the blood from Marty's face, neck, and hands.

"You think anything's broken?" he asks.

"Just head," Marty grunts. The wet cloth toweling his fingers is soothing. He relaxes and lets himself be sponged. The cloth combs through his beard and hair. The smell of blood dissolves. Instead, he inhales the fresh, clean, warm water and the faint, intoxicating odor of disinfectant. Finally, the cloth reaches a corner of his forehead.

"Aww," Marty moans. He has a low tolerance for pain.

The guard has not yet touched the wound, but he proceeds delicately. "Bad cut," he concurs. "But the bleeding has stopped."

"That's good." Anya says. Her fright has nearly dissipated.

"Head wounds always bleed a lot," the guard says expertly. "Sometimes it ain't nothing, but it can still look like you got ripped apart by a dog."

The sergeant hands an ice-pack to the guard who places it gingerly on Marty's forehead.

"Awawww, awawaa," Marty groans again and swivels his neck so the bag of ice falls to the floor.

His eyes light on a list of Allowable Items:

> *Tissue Pack unopened*
> *Two Keys On A Ring with No Attachments*
> *Six Disposable Diapers*
> *One Single-Layer Burp Cloth*

"Burp cloth," he mutters.

The guard lays the ice-pack back on Marty's head. "You gotta be brave, big guy," he cajoles.

Marty grimaces. He knows he doesn't have to be anything.

"Where can we go now?" Anya asks.

"Where were you going?" the sergeant eyes her lasciviously.

Anya shrugs. She never knows.

"But weren't you on your way somewhere?"

"I mean," she stutters. She is expert at avoiding explanations. Most survivors are. "What about stitches?"

"That's what I'm saying," the attending guard explains. "It's nothing. A head wound looks bad because it's bloody. It feels bad because it hurts. He can get stitches if he's worried about a scar. But if I was him," he looks at Marty's fleshy ball of face, the untidy copper-colored beard, the bushy eyebrows, the flabby eyelids, the dandruff in the lashes, and the irritated red complexion, "I wouldn't worry about it. Keep the ice on. It's going to heal fine."

He gently presses the worm-shaped globule of blood that binds the wound itself. A thick sap-like layer has formed on the surface.

"Excellent vitamin K," he pronounces and slaps Marty's thigh.

"Sounds like everything's fine," the sergeant says cheerfully. Although it has been an unusual night, rules have only been adjusted, not broken. And there has been no disaster.

Relief floods Marty with a sense of well-being. "I wonder if you got clothes I can buy," he asks. He plucks at the blood-stiff sleeves of his jacket. Blood stains his khaki trousers, his striped rugby shirt, even his undershirt. "Anything at all, I buy it."

"What the hell we going to sell you? One of them prison uniforms?" The sergeant cracks himself up.

"I was thinking maybe," Marty stumbles. His thinking is not so clear. "Maybe somebody recently died and you still have clothes."

"No, no, buddy," the sergeant says vehemently. "Somebody dies, every last thing he brought in here goes out with his body back to the family. We don't have a right to keep nothing. That is strictly prohibited." He adds knowingly, "Punishable as theft."

"We can buy something up the road," Anya chimes in.

"What about those suitcases?" The sergeant scrutinizes his two guests. He wonders if he ought not to be more suspicious. It's a fine line between caution and paranoia, and he tells himself he must proceed carefully.

"There's only my personal valise," Anya admits.

"Valise?" The sergeant imitates her accent. He is barely familiar with the term and can see his teasing has not pleased her. "So you ain't got any men's clothing in your valise?" He haws, "Where your cousin put his pajamas?" Winking at the guards. "He probably don't wear pajamas."

Foolish questions and silly comments make Marty nervous. He doesn't like snooping. He doesn't like questions. He passes Anya a reproachful look. It's a reminder she should keep her mouth shut at all times.

"What's in those other suitcases we saw back there?" The sergeant's eyes narrow.

The guard dabs Marty's head with alcohol. Marty winces with the cold burn of pain while Anya blows on the cut.

"Are you sure he doesn't need stitches?" Anya does her best to sound concerned.

There's an uncomfortable silence.

One of the guards has found coveralls in the janitor's closet. He helps Marty change into the uniform and stuffs his bloody clothes into a plastic bag.

"So," the sergeant announces, "I am personally going to escort you back to your vehicle. That sound good to you?" He leers at Anya with a lopsided smile.

Marty manages to wag his aching head. "Thank you," he says sincerely.

"Anyways I got to check your gun license before I hand this pretty little thing back to you." He slips the SIG into his pocket. It's so light he can barely feel it.

"Can you walk?" Anya asks.

Marty shades his eyes away from the overhead fluorescent tubes. When he stands up, he feels faint. He can't remember ever feeling so bad, except an accident in Moscow that followed a car chase. It ended in a bad crash and still gives him nightmares.

14

Marty slips off the gurney. "I would like to walk out," he says affably. It's a superstition from the year he spent in a Russian prison.

He hangs between Anya's hand and the sergeant's elbow. The damp and chilly pre-dawn air is refreshing. There's a long hoot of an owl. In the distance the black outline of high hills are etched against the black night. The wind whips the loose dirt beside the driveway.

"Everything okay?" José is outside the Visitors Center on a cigarette break.

"Perfect," Anya smiles demurely. She catches Marty's glare that suggests she's overdoing it. "Absolutely perfect," she says with spite.

The sergeant orders José to take Marty's arm in his stead. The trio shuffles towards the parking lot with the sergeant leading the way. A dozen eucalyptus saplings have been planted by the cement walk as well as a border of California wild lilac not quite in bloom.

After Marty is helped into the back of the van, he directs Anya to the attaché case behind him. It is stashed beneath her suitcase and a couple of small duffles.

"So what's in them?" the sergeant asks. "Ain't some of his clothes in there?" He winks over at José.

Anya removes the attaché case. Marty tries to rotate the correct sequence of numbers for the lock, but his fingers are weak and clumsy. He curses in Russian under his breath.

"You open it then," the sergeant says to Anya.

She gazes into the field. A small fuzzy shape catches her eye. She watches it creep slowly across the barren ground, then disappear into a ditch.

"I have to open it," Marty says unnerved.

"Don't trust your cousin?" This time he winks at Anya.

Finally, the lock snaps open.

Inside are piles of loose documents. Most of them forged identity papers, passports, and work permits for the girls. There are also stacks of banded hundred-dollar bills and euros. Marty burrows into the papers and pulls out the gun license.

"No *problema*," the sergeant says, inspecting the date and handing the gun over to Marty. Then, he surveys the large number of official-looking documents and extravagant amounts of cash, both US and foreign.

"What kind of business you in?"

"I'm lawyer," Marty responds. It's a title that usually serves to intimidate anyone.

The sergeant, however, is not intimidated. In the difficult business of law enforcement, attorneys and journalists are the lowest forms of vermin.

"So you got a client up there?" The sergeant furiously jerks his head back to the prison. "Thought you'd stop by and get yourself an up-front, personal look at the joint, huh? We didn't treat you good enough, huh?"

Marty clamps shut the attaché case and slips it under the seat. He motions to Anya to get into the car.

"You're on my property," the sergeant declares.

Marty nods respectfully. "Do not worry. I'm not such kind of lawyer," he tries to say. "We off property in less than one minute." He waves Anya on.

The sergeant is overheated. "If I got a problem with something, I can look at whatever I want. That's the law." He pats his badge.

Marty wavers between silence and protest. He knows better but like the sergeant, sometimes he can't help himself. Sometimes he loses patience. He dares another attempt at intimidation.

"Not unless you get search warrant," Marty counters.

"You wanna search warrant?" the sergeant threatens. However, he does not plan to wait. The money, the papers, the gun have aroused his suspicions. Reasonable suspicions, he tells himself. This lawyer has violated his hospitality.

He yanks Anya's valise from the back of the van and pitches it and the duffle bags onto the pavement.

José is on alert.

"Get your wetback Mexican ass over here," the sergeant commands. "Open it."

José tugs at the zipper of the black duffle.

"Dump it."

The sergeant expects to find the devices that all devious lawyers carry into prisons. He expects to see miniature recording machines, miniature cameras hidden inside pens, invisible ink, infra-red goggles.

However, tumbling around his feet is another sort of paraphernalia: colorful dildos, triple-prong vibrators, leather leotards, leather masks, shackles such as chains, handcuffs, ropes, riding whips, crops, ticklers such as French and otherwise, panties with slits in the crotch, bustiers and garters, seamed stockings, wigs, boxes of makeup, and baggies filled with costume jewelry.

The sergeant whistles through his teeth as he and José ogle the items. Some, they recognize. Others, they can't identify. They are simultaneously disgusted and aroused, filled with judgments and desire.

Anya stands by indifferently. She knows there will be a few stupid questions. Marty will tell her to pick up the things, put them back into the bags, and then they will drive away. Marty will blame her, and she will tell him to fuck off. It once happened outside Houston when they got stopped for speeding.

"No *problema,*" Anya mutters to break the silence. It is an agreeable, universally understood expression she has often heard Pedro say. Pedro! The two simple syllables peal through her brain. She cannot imagine what has happened to Pedro. A picture of his hairy spider body appears. Reflexively, she starts to laugh. At first, they are giggles but soon the girlish sounds turn to something riotous and uncontrolled.

It is the picture of a large spider body groping through the fog that amuses her. Pedro is trying to find them, but they have vanished. The car has vanished. Pedro rubs his eyes. He pinches his hairy arms. She can see his dumb expression. He cannot believe it. It simply can't be true. This is precisely what's funny: the picture of Pedro trotting up and down the gully in the fog, hopelessly, pointlessly, uselessly.

Anya's laughs are so wild she must stop and gasp for breath. She almost chokes.

"Tell her to shut up," the sergeant turns to Marty.

Marty says nothing. There is nothing to say. He has learned through experience. These things happen. They are unexpected and unpleasant, but in a very short time, they sort themselves out.

"Tell her to shut up."

The sound of the sergeant's voice only incites her. Anya is still laughing when he jams a dildo in her mouth and twists her arms behind her back.

15

osé is ready to call back the guards. He looks for a signal from the sergeant, but the sergeant is preoccupied with Anya's things. He is sorting through the articles of women's clothing: the diaphanous nightgowns, the saucy brassieres, the minute miniskirts and sheer blouses, the slips and tiny thongs. He picks up one thing and another.

Most of the scattered objects on the ground José has seen in the back pages of girlie magazines. He assiduously peruses the ads in fine print. These tidbits of information tempt him with delectable, exquisite, and secret pleasures. He has noted the smaller the ad, the more esoteric the pleasure. He wrestles with his desires. He confesses at church. To date, he has never had the nerve to place an order.

Unfortunately, the negligees are too familiar. José has seen them hanging off chairs and hooks in the one room he shared with his mother. They lived in Guat City in a fourth-rate bordello. Whenever a man was with her, José was put outside the door to wait in the hall until she was finished.

"You wanna get out of here? Or would you rather come back inside?" the sergeant asks, removing the dildo from Anya's mouth and throwing it on the asphalt. He can feel his extremities swelling with omnipotence. The upper hand is all his.

Anya is silent.

"Show him your tongue," Marty calls out from the backseat.

Anya opens her lips, sticks her tongue out like a cobra. The pink muscle flips from one side to the other; curls in like a taco; rolls back into a ball; and with a twist squeezes again into the head of a cobra.

"Titties," Marty shouts.

With disinterest, Anya undoes the covered fake-fur buttons of her coat. She yanks the low-cut scoop of sweater down below her bra. The large, creamy upper halves of her breasts are visible above the lacy demi-cups. The areolas of two salmon-colored nipples beckon from beneath a swatch of turquoise lace.

The sergeant unzips his pants and awkwardly unfolds his member. Anya kicks off her high heels and squats at the level of his waist so he can slide himself between her breasts. She kneads her flesh around the sides of his penis, enfolding it until only the tip is visible.

The sergeant observes from above. It is only two feet, but it feels like a great height. A spectacular aerial view over an inviolable law. Not his law but nature's: women are born to satisfy men.

He watches while Anya's softness heaves and swallows his hardness. A rush of admiration for his tip fills him: its swollen pink dome punctuated by the speck of a hole. He watches adoringly as it rides up and down along the bone of her sternum.

Anya swings back on her heels and pulls her breasts completely out of their cups. Her firm, round fullness is exposed. She pulls his pants down to his knees, takes him into her palm. She guides it like a gear shift around each orb of breast. She drums him on her nipples. They harden, and she squashes him back and forth in the drops of his own jism. Then, she replaces the hard cylinder back inside the folds of flesh.

José is hypnotized. He wants to kill the sergeant. This is his deepest and most ancient feeling. Beneath the alcove of a hall in a bordello in Guatemala, he made little ambuscades. He made them with a dirty sheet. Inside, he stashed sticks for guns, a clown mask for disguise. There he planned the killings. He killed every man who came out of his mother's room.

José's eyes water with despair. He touches the gun in its holster. No more sticks. It's a real gun. He fingers the trigger and releases the safety.

The raw, sweaty crack in the sergeant's ass is a perfect target, but it is moving. It requires good aim. José has neither training nor practice. He would like to blow away the sergeant's ass, but it constantly jiggles up and down. First, he is on his flat feet. Then, like a ballerina he rises on his toes. Whether up or down, he is always jabbing his body forward at the girl's chest. He jabs as if he plans to drill a hole through her rib-cage.

Once in a while, Marty checks outside the van. He appreciates Anya's good sportsmanship. He cranes his neck so he can watch. In her tight jeans, Anya's legs and buttocks are still superb, but the rest has gotten too thin. Her breasts have lost some plump and look punctured. Her slim, luscious waist is bony. And her pelvis protrudes.

Marty collapses back on the seat. It hurts to move, but he feels better. In the janitor's coveralls, he feels relatively clean. He tries to recall the accident. He remembers the fog dropping like a stage curtain. He remembers the squeal of brakes and the nearly invisible center divide.

However, he cannot remember what has happened to Pedro. Was he thrown from the vehicle? Does that mean Pedro is dead? Is his body lying on top of a stinking shit pie with the cows? Or is he injured, waiting for them to find him?

Marty is sorry if that is the case, but at least the van is unscathed. And despite the blood and pain, his injury is minor. He is grateful. Best of all, Anya is unharmed and can still deliver.

He wonders, however, what could she have possibly been thinking to bring them to a prison. Maybe she planned to report him and turn him in. Kidnaping, trafficking, rape, these are not minor charges. They carry severe consequences. But Anya wouldn't be stupid enough to entrust herself to the law. The sergeant's behavior only proves his point. Obviously, he reasons, she hoped to seek help for him. Marty sighs. He is gladdened to think her intentions were pure.

> *The less we love her, the more surely*
> *We stand to gain a woman's heart*

He, like Pushkin's hero Onegin, is glad for the unfathomable singular mystery of women. Unless one is inclined to drink, it alone makes life bearable.

Marty checks through the window. Anya remains on her haunches, and the sergeant is still riding up and down. He peers at the man's flat, formless ass and the red pimples that dot both cheeks. They remind him of a target too.

Wearily, Anya punches her breasts against the sergeant's penis. She drools on her hands. With the drool she rubs his navel, his belly, his loins. She strokes his dick with her slippery fingers, her hand, her nipples, her breasts. She slips her contorted tongue onto the end of his engorged member and coaxes him in a breathless whisper, "Baby, baby."

The sergeant hears her words from far away. He holds onto his hardness.

"Come, baby," she insists. Some men like insistence, even men in uniforms.

A stream of spittle falls from the sergeant's mouth onto the top of Anya's hair. She feels it trickling on her temples and over her ears. His juts grow harder and rougher.

Again, she takes him inside her mouth and twirls her tongue up and down the shaft. How many minutes has it been? She wonders.

"Big guy," she utters.

The sergeant hears these words too, but they are not so distant. He is falling, and her words, her tits, her hair are catching him. He is falling and reaching at the same time. Soon he will be safe. He will have reached across the gulf between one long drawn-out pleasure and a second more intense, more inexorable pleasure.

He grasps his own throat with his hand. Then, as the pressure valve starts to discharge over Anya's breasts, through her hair and on her face, a shot rings out.

16

"Bloody fuck," Marty says, staring out at the spot where the sergeant just stood.

Anya crawls across the asphalt. "What happened?" She screams.

"For fuck's sake, shut up," Marty commands. "Get in van."

A bewildered Anya looks for her friend, the one they call Beaner. He is not there. He has disappeared, and a body is now lying in the visitors' parking lot.

The little shadow Anya saw earlier in the field has crept boldly onto the pavement. It's a gray kitten. It purrs and runs to Anya's side. It licks Anya's toes and purrs again.

"Get in," she hears Marty yelling.

Anya sticks her breasts back into her bra, wipes her face with her sweater, buttons her coat, and climbs behind the steering wheel.

"Now drive fuck out of here."

"What about the stuff?"

Marty gestures. "Forget stuff."

Forget? Anya can't forget. She likes stuff. In her life, she finally has stuff. A few pretty things are the only compensation.

"I want my pearls," she says defiantly.

"Anya, shut up." Marty points out the window. "You want live rest of life in place like that?"

"Mr. Kupkin gave me those pearls."

"They ain't real Anya so it don't matter. They ain't real pearls."

Anya turns over the ignition. In the side mirror she looks lovingly at the pile of nighties, jewelry, wigs. These are the things she earned with her own body. She chokes back a sob. Somehow they've become more precious than her body.

Marty leans forward. He can smell the ammonia traces of semen in her hair. "Anya, stop thinking about shit that don't matter." He takes a towel from the back and hands it over to her. "Clean your hair."

At the side of the van, the kitten drags a French tickler across the driveway, flings the ring of rubber from its mouth, and ferociously pounces on it.

Anya backs the van away from the sergeant's body, rolls over a dozen dildos, stops, leans like an acrobat out the door, and grabs the kitten. She makes a wide semi-circle with the van and floors the accelerator, racing to the road that connects them back to I-5.

Marty stares through the back window. There are no floodlights or sirens. There is only quiet darkness. The simple outline of buildings and black hills. Except for the rolls of razor wire and high fences, it is nearly picturesque.

Anya is nervous. She nearly loses control.

"We don't need fucking traffic ticket," Marty warns her.

Anya hits the brakes. The speedometer drops from 90 to 45. "Which way?" she asks.

They head north, retracing the miles they traveled over an hour ago. The kitten curls on Anya's lap. Marty leans his throbbing head back against the seat. He has to think good, he tells himself. He has to ask all the right questions and come up with the right answers.

"Did you shoot him?" Anya timidly asks.

"You think I lost fucking mind?"

Anya considers the question seriously. She has to admit that while Marty appears to be an even-tempered man, she believes he is capable of anything.

"Then, who shot him?"

"How fuck should I know, Anya? But if fuckhead has even pea for brain, he'll tell them it was us."

"You think?"

"Anya, you ain't stupid. We both sitting," he stutters, "sitting ducks, you and me. Think about it. Didn't your *dedushka* used to hunt ducks? Didn't he go out at dawn and shoot when they come up from marsh? Think about it, Anya. Those ducks weren't sitting. They were flying, and he still bagged few. But us, we might as well be dead for what they do to aliens that wipe out police person."

Anya shudders. After *babushka*, her grandfather was her favorite person. *Dedushka* loved jokes. He told jokes and played jokes. Whenever he teased Anya and made her cry, he took her on his lap and tickled her chin until she stopped crying. He said his jokes only meant he loved her. After Ba fell into the hole the plane made, her grandfather forgot all his jokes. He sat in the corner of the house all day and smoked. They had to make him eat. They had to make him bathe. He stank all the time. He slept on a mattress on the floor in Anya's room, and when she was asleep, she could smell him. One morning she woke up, and her grandfather was hanging from a beam. His tongue was completely black and his eyes completely white.

Now she can't recall if he ever hunted ducks. Her dead grandfather and grandmother, her brother, her little sisters, the town, the farm, the river, the dogs, even something as simple as ducks belong to a world far away. Anya thinks not her but another person, a young, lost, beautiful person, must have lived there once and then died herself.

"What we going to do, Marty?" Anya cries.

Across the valley to the east, a streak of pink flutters like tissue paper above the gray clouds and the high crests of the snow-capped Sierra.

"What we going to do?"

Marty doesn't answer. He is thinking. He is thinking good. He tries to decipher the most pertinent questions: did the cocksucker who shot the motherfucker run away? Or did he alert the other cocksuckers? Everything depends on the answers to these two questions, but they're imponderable.

He scans the highway behind them. No sirens, no police cars, no chase. He looks over the fallow, empty fields and the web of small roads that diverge to the east. Wisps of fog drift and disappear like smoke.

"I bet this where we run into fog," he finally says.

On the east side of I-5, fresh parallel tracks of ruts cut a diagonal on the unpaved shoulder. The wet weeds have recently been flattened, and there are several additional tracks of backward and forward movements.

"And Pedro?" Marty sighs regretfully. "Disappearing like that. It don't make sense."

Anya had forgotten about Pedro.

"I wish there time to look for body, but there ain't. Anyways," he considers, "he ain't got ID. No way they trace him to us."

"That's good," Anya says. It seems he has already disappeared for Marty too. "I never liked him."

"I know, but it don't matter now so keep nasty thoughts to yourself."

"They aren't nasty thoughts. They got nothing to do with nasty."

"He was good driver, Anya." Marty pictures Pedro's small, shriveled hairy body and vivid raisin face. "He didn't ask questions. He didn't complain. You give Pedro piece of stale bread, he happy. Anya, you don't remember happiness for a crumb because you spoiled. Pedro never changed. Nothing ever spoiled him."

Marty is a man who prides himself on understanding human nature. He says human nature is the subject of his life-long investigation. He thinks he's an authority.

Marty tries to maintain a rapport with all the girls. He brings them little gifts. He quotes them poems in Russian. If they don't speak Russian, he quotes the poems anyway because he says it sounds poetic. On their birthdays, he brings them flowers. If they got problems, he listens. If they're sad, it's his shoulder they can cry on. If they get homesick, they can talk to him.

Marty makes Anya write to her Ba. Like a good girl she writes on the first Sunday. Sabbath ritual. He reads the letters. He makes sure there's nothing desperate in them. Usually, they make him smile. Descriptions of her job in a florist shop, her nice apartment with a dishwasher, fresh oranges she can buy everyday, all-you-can-eat restaurants, things all Russian people love. At the beginning and end of each letter Anya writes, *Pray for me.* That's the only part that disturbs him. He can't fathom what it means. *Pray for me.* After he reads the letter, he seals it. He carries them with his personal belongings in the leather kit with his toothbrush. That's where he puts Anya's letters to her Ba.

"All I said was I didn't like him. It isn't that complicated."

"But you don't like nothing, Anya. You don't like nobody. Pedro, he was harmless. He was pitiful. But you don't take pity on nobody or nothing."

Anya does not respond. Why should she? She does her job. She's a model employee. Even Mr. Kupkin says so.

Anya prefers a straightforward tyrant. Kupkin is clear about his job and hers. He's clear about everything. She has respect for Kupkin. He's not a hypocrite like Marty. Why should she care what a hypocrite thinks? Marty only wants her trust so he can control her. She sees through that. She understands his kind of enlightenment. He uses his so-called compassion for control.

Tenderly, she massages the kitten's back and ears. It purrs and burrows deeper against her belly. She massages the tiny, crackling bones in its neck. When it purrs, she purrs in return. All her love collects in her fingertips and disperses into the kitten. That's proof of love, she thinks. Proof of true, true love.

17

Anya asks Marty if he hears a sound. "That noise," she insists. Marty doesn't hear anything. All his attention is concentrated on the rear window.

"Off freeway, next exit," Marty says. He thinks he's thinking good, but he's not sure.

NO SERVICES is indicated on the sign. Reluctantly, Anya takes the exit. There are no lights visible in either direction. When they get to the end of the ramp, she asks Marty which way.

"How I know?" He snaps. He looks to the right towards the mountains. Mountains have an appeal. He looks left. There are mountains too, closer, not so high, and without snow.

"Right," he finally says.

Thoughts crowd Marty's mind. He needs a plan. He needs a different car, some water, a few crackers, and a couple hours of sleep. Then, he could make what he calls an informed decision. Marty's brain is starting to whirl. By now they've certainly found the dead or wounded man with his pants down. Maybe even the lunatic who shot him. At least, Anya knows how to drive. At least, she wasn't shot. Marty can't believe it was the Mexican guard, but that's the only reasonable assumption. At least, she drives not too bad, he thinks. Maybe the way is clear, he thinks. So far, no one is coming, no one is looking. So far, no one cares.

No assumptions, Marty reminds himself. That's how he has gotten this far.

Anya slams on the brakes. The thump of a heavy object against metal is heard from underneath the bench in the back where luggage can be stored.

"I told you," she shrieks.

Marty pulls his gun from under the seat.

"Don't shoot me," a voice cries, a vaguely familiar voice.

"Come out," Marty demands.

"I told you," Anya says.

"You drive, shut up," he tells her.

The man's arms emerge, raised over his head. Before Marty sees his face, he sees his uniform.

"It's Mexican lunatic," he says to Anya.

"Not Mexican."

"Put him out," she suggests.

"José," Marty recalls.

"Not José."

"Not José, not Mexican," Marty muses. "But killer?"

The guard lowers his eyes. He is aware he has committed a mortal sin, but it was not for nothing.

"It was not for nothing," he says aloud. "I had a good reason. He attacked your cousin. Is that not reason?"

"What does he say?" Anya calls out.

"He did for you," Marty says ruefully.

Anya turns around and smiles.

"It wasn't no favor," Marty exclaims. "Police looking for us, van, him. They think maybe we kidnap him. They think we kill police person and kidnap José."

"My name is Gervasio," the young guard says insistently. "I come from Guatemala."

Marty holds his head which feels as if it's falling off. "But they call you 'José?'"

"They tell me my name's too long. They change my name to José."

"Nobody likes Mexicans," Anya says.

"I'm not Mexican."

"Same thing." She has absorbed a loathing of Mexicans. She doesn't know how. Maybe because Marty says they're not good for business, either as clients or whores. Blacks, she likes. She finds them beautiful. Marty tells her Russians like black-skinned people because of Pushkin's great grandfather, Abram Petrovich Gannibal. He was African.

"So you blew him away?"

Gervasio nods. "I don't aim. I only shoot. Perhaps there's a chance he still lives."

"And you jumped in van?"

"He was raping the lady," Gervasio explains.

"You tell them. You see what they say," Marty grins maliciously.

"Then, you come with me," Gervasio pleads. "You tell them what happened to your cousin."

"You crazy. You know what they do to us?"

Gervasio has his own logic. "I stopped a crime. That is what they trained me to do."

"They didn't train you. They told you to stand all night in Visitors Center," Marty says.

The truth is a painful reminder. "Take me," Gervasio's voice catches in a sob.

"We can't take you. We give you something to wear, then you go out there." Marty waves the gun at the back window.

There's a gray field with a windbreak of dark, leafless trees. A small clearing where farm equipment is parked.

"Pull over," Marty says to Anya.

"What you doing?" she asks cautiously. She doesn't want to stop in the middle of nowhere. The orchard reminds her of a drawing in a children's book. A place where the witch Baba-Yaga lives with her flying pestle and flying broom.

"I don't like it here, Marty." Anya shivers.

"Get something him wear, anything. Jeans, shirt. Something." Marty grabs his attaché case and sifts through the papers. He lifts out a Brazilian passport and rips out the photograph.

"Fonseca," he says. "You like name? That your name."

Anya has found a pair of sweat pants and sweat shirt under the seat. Both lavender. She hands them to Marty.

"Okay, we go now into there," he points his gun into the dark orchard. Marty holds the passport and hundred-dollar bill. "You change clothes."

Gervasio takes the clothing from Anya.

"One minute," Marty tells her.

Fifty yards into the orchard, Gervasio strips off his uniform.

"I take for you," Marty picks up the pants, jacket, and shirt. "I dump for you. You walk," he waves the gun. "Maybe we get lucky."

As he hands the passport to Gervasio, he shoots once into the left side of his chest. Marty thinks it's the gun, not his aim. The gun is a perfect instrument. He throws the money onto the corpse.

Anya has heard the shot. It's cold. She wraps a shirt around her neck for warmth. She is trembling when Marty returns to the van.

"Turn around," he says. "Get fuck out."

Anya drives.

"What?" Marty finally asks.

Anya says nothing.

"What you want? He could tell them anything. He could tell them we used his gun to kill police person. Anyways what you think? When facts come out, José kaput. He already dead man, tortured and then dead. They put needle in the arm and poison in the body. You enjoy idea?"

Marty considers it a favor. He doesn't like to kill, not even pigeons or cats like other boys used to do. He has only killed two men. Both in self-defense. This too was a kind of self-defense, he thinks. Mercy-killing too, he thinks.

Anya says nothing. Everything makes her sick, Marty most of all.

18

At the juncture of Highway 33 and 180, Pedro appears like a ghost.

"Thank fucking Jesus," Marty sings out as the van slows down.

A petrified grin has frozen on Pedro's face. It hangs from ear to ear. Two stained buck teeth and a pair of closely set, saucer-shaped eyes completely fill his face. A cropped cap of tiny curls covers his head, and his downy ears stick out like wind flaps.

"You ain't dead," Marty shouts jubilantly as he slides open the door and pulls Pedro into the van. "Pedro the Tarantula lives!"

Pedro is stunned. He cannot speak. Over the last couple of hours, a reunion with Marty and Anya has decreased to a vast improbability. He has calculated that if such an improbability were to become reality, it would be nothing short of miraculous.

"Pedro," Marty consoles. He puts his arms around the bony shoulders and embraces the small, underclad body tightly against his chest.

Pedro crosses himself several times and mutters prayers to the Virgin of Guadalupe, the Holy Father, and his mother who died from a heart attack in a strawberry field. Then helplessly, he starts to weep large, violent sobs.

"Shush," Marty soothes Pedro's shaking frame. "Ssshhh, ssshhh, we here now."

"Where were you?" Pedro stutters.

"He don't want to know," Marty laughs cheerlessly. Then adds, "We been in long, bad dream."

Anya is grim.

"You missed it." Marty slaps his own thigh as evidence. "That's first piece of luck since we picked you out of garbage can."

Pedro stops sobbing. Like so many other moments in his life, everything seems different and everything seems the same. He notes the blood-soaked gauze on Marty's forehead and the brown coveralls whose arms are too short. Missing is Marty's striped rugby shirt and khaki pants.

"Why you wearing that?" he asks.

Marty pats the cut on his forehead. The bleeding has stopped. "This all I could find."

Pedro grins as if he understands. "I got real hungry standing out there." He pulls a bag from under the front seat. "Half the time, all I think about is little banana. Other half, I think about you."

"We're hungry too," Anya complains.

Reluctantly, Pedro breaks off pieces of the banana.

The sky is dirty white and misty. Fields stretch out on both sides of road. An apricot orchard is bare and black on the white horizon. There is little traffic: a school bus, a few cars, an open truck of farm laborers. There are sporadic clusters of houses and trailers. Here and there, a cow stands in the cold or horses prance exuberantly. A wind covers the windshield with a film of rust-colored dust.

Marty checks the map. "33 to 152."

Anya is skeptical. She doesn't like the empty fields and little houses. She has lived in rooms for almost four years. Open space scares her. It looks dirty and stupid. Most of all, she doesn't like to drive slow. If you have to get away, better to go fast. Better to go fast and make a mistake than poke around in the dirt.

Marty opens his attaché case and removes a few hundred-dollar bills. From a small enamel box, he takes out two aspirins, two anti-inflammatories, and a wake-up pill which he sticks down his throat. He can barely make saliva in his parched mouth. His thirst is overwhelming.

"My kingdom for glass of water," Marty waves the money.

At the next intersection is a filling station. Its two pumps look old, unused. A mid-size rental truck is parked off to the side. Marty orders Anya out of the car to get him something to drink.

"Tell Pedro to do it," she objects.

"Pedro is cold." Marty laughs. The wake-up pill has started to perk him up. "Pedro had bad night."

Anya checks her reflection. Deep circles eclipse her eyes. Her hair is matted and uncombed, her face dirty and bruised. She buttons her coat and sticks the kitten in the pocket.

"Ask if you get cup of something," Marty waves her on.

"It's too early," she protests but moves forward.

Through a grime-coated window, Anya sees two men. One is black, the other white. Engrossed with several loose sheets of paper, they're seated next to the red coils of an electric heater. The white man holds a clipboard. The black man sips a cup of steaming liquid.

When Anya knocks, the man shoves his clipboard into the drawer of a desk. He points to two big orange signs: CLOSED and BEWARE OF DOG.

"Dog?" Anya tentatively asks, clamping her hand around the kitten as she opens the door.

The room smells like weak coffee. Dust covers the metal counter and the floor. Strings of cobwebs hang from the ceiling.

"No gas," the men say. "*Comprende?* Closed. No gas." They point to the old pumps and look out at the late-model van with tinted windows. "Go back to I-5. *Comprende?*"

Anya shakes her head and leans against the door.

"Water," she finally says as if she had staggered across a desert.

"That we got," the black man says affably. He returns from a back room with a paper cup of tepid water.

Anya drinks the contents in one gulp. She holds out the cup, "Please?"

The cup is filled again.

They watch as Anya totters on high heels, sloshing half the contents of the cup over the cracked asphalt.

Inside the van Marty sips his precious water. The taste is sour but any liquid will suffice.

"What's in there?" he asks.

Pedro has replaced Anya in the driver's seat.

"You hear me?" Marty spits.

"Nothing," she says. "Nothing is in there."

"What about truck?"

Anya shrugs. "Nothing."

"You turn stupid or what? We still in trouble case you don't remember."

Anya is indifferent. Trouble enough is hunger and fatigue. Anything else is extraneous.

"I told Pedro what happened."

Anya's non-existent eyebrows rise quizzically.

"We got to dump van." Marty points his finger at the truck. "Where it going?"

"How the fuck should I know?" Anya cries indignantly. "I went to get you water. Two gentlemen are drinking their morning coffee. I didn't ask their life story. You want their life story? You ask them."

Marty beckons Anya to the backseat. "You cranky and tired. Lie down."

Instantly, Anya collapses into a fitful sleep with the kitten tucked in her arms. Through her sleep, she hears the duet of a rooster and a dog. The shrill doodle reminds Anya of her brother on the morning they took him away. And the bark, the voices of the secret police calling his name from the street.

"Dima," they barked. When he sleepily appeared, they handcuffed him and threw him into an unmarked car. The family was not allowed to visit him. They were told he was suspected of terrorist activities in Groznii. Their pleas went unheeded although they swore Dimitri was not a rebel. Nor were they Muslims. A month later, Anya's mother received notice she could pick up his body at the prison. The death certificate stated he died of a heart attack. There were red welts around his neck, cigarette burns up and down his arms.

Anya was almost eighteen when Dima died. Afterwards, she was consumed day and night with leaving. She plotted how far her small savings could take her and what she might do along the way. Her education was decent. She read and wrote well. She spoke some English, some French. She was good with numbers. She had ambitions to get her teeth fixed and become a fashion model in an European capital. She possessed photogenic qualities. She was pretty, blond, slender, buxom, and a little bold.

Mr. Kupkin appeared like a genie. He invited her to work in the United States. She told her mother, "It's a miracle that a nice, rich Russian man wants Russian girls to work in his restaurants."

Kupkin's terms were uncomplicated. He paid Anya's mother $1,800 to compensate for her lost earnings over a period of six months. He carried a document for her mother to sign, authorizing himself as guardian. He bought Anya, her mother, and two younger sisters new clothes. He procured a passport from the OVIR. He bought her an airline ticket to Atlanta. He explained she would initially train and work there, but as soon as he opened other restaurants, Anya could have her choice of California, Texas, or New York. At first, she would not receive a wage. At first, she would have to reimburse Kupkin for her expenses. After that, Anya's mother would start receiving a portion of her earnings. Eventually, there would be enough for Anya to send for other members of her family.

The rooster is now quiet, but the barking dog continues to disturb Anya's sleep. She dreams of her brother: his warm, sleepy face and long, disheveled hair. His prized American blue jeans that he stole.

After a quarter of an hour, a tall, lanky black man sticks his head out the door of the deserted gas station. He is surprised to see the van still parked by the defunct pumps.

"You lost or something?" He asks, chewing the end of an unlit thin cigar.

"Got lost," Marty confirms.

The man points to the road. "Straight to I-5."

"Van broken," Marty adds, inspecting the man's pressed cowboy shirt, leather jacket, and baseball cap.

"Lost and broken down," he nods with the understanding of a veteran of the road. "What's wrong with it?"

Marty searches for a plausible response.

"Cracked block," Pedro says expertly.

"You run out of oil or something?"

Marty wags his head.

The man takes in the threesome: a sleeping, unkempt girl, a fat, bandaged head on a man holding an attaché case with gilt initials, and a small, hairy youth who can't stop shaking. His instincts are overridden by his conscience.

"Where you going?" Marty dares to ask. Thirty hundred-dollar bills ripple through his hands. "We got to get to Oakland," Marty smiles. "For appointment." The gums show around his broken upper teeth. A familiar feeling swells in his chest. Theatrically, he fans the money.

Recognition flickers across the black cowboy's face. He knows he saw the movie, but he can't recall where. He regards the money and the fat head. Delicately, he lowers the thin cigar from his mouth and presses the stub into the ground with the tip of his polished cowboy boot.

Marty takes it as a sign. "Maybe we leave van in garage." Now he is thinking, thinking good. "We pay thousand dollar rent for month and two thousand," he searches for the word, "for transport."

The man scratches his head thoughtfully. "It's enough."

19

On the dashboard of the truck Mohammed has placed a few religious magnets: a cross, a Saint Christopher, a Buddha, a Jewish star. Hanging from the rearview mirror are an eagle feather, a string of prayer beads, and a large button with the face of Bob Marley. In addition, photographs of children, also magnets, cling to the dash.

Mohammed guides the truck around the island of gas pumps onto the road. The ride is surprisingly smooth, surprisingly comfortable.

Marty sighs with relief as the garage recedes. The van is not in sight. It's a new day, he reminds himself. The terrible night is behind them.

They travel in silence. Pedro and Marty doze. Anya stares ahead. She fingers the top of the kitten's head, but truthfully she feels nearly dead. Every sensation is deadened. She is no longer hungry or tired, no longer anxious or frightened. She feels nothing except the total absence of feeling. Even the bare empty fields are no longer ominous, only sad.

"Where you from?" Mohammed speaks softly, the words barely distinguishable from the din of tires rolling forward.

"Russia," Marty starts from his sleep.

Mohammed looks admiringly at Anya. "You too?"

"Far from home," Mohammed laughs gently.

Anya likes his laugh. It spills out of his mouth like the treble of a piano. It is gentle, warm.

"I guess we're all far from home," he adds. "I'm far in both space and time. You know what I mean?"

Neither Anya nor Marty knows what he means but shake their heads in agreement.

"Sometimes it feels I been gone a thousand years." Mohammed laughs again. "You know what I mean?"

This time Anya does understand. She has been gone that long too and knows she's never going back.

Mohammed waves at the passing vehicles. Everyone waves back.

"Why do they wave?" Anya asks.

"They know I am Number Three Son of the First Man." He kisses his thumb and reaches over to the cross, the Magen David, the prayer beads.

Anya wonders if he is gifted or crazy. She has never heard of a number three son. She has only heard of Moses, Abel, Cain, and Jesus.

Instead of west on 152, Mohammed turns right, due east towards Highway 99.

"A little errand," he says.

"How long?" Marty asks disgruntled.

"Travel time is short but waiting can kill you. That's one thing I know." He smiles gratefully at Anya. "Company helps pass the wait."

Marty regards the backside of the black prophet's well-shaped head. It recalls the pimpled ass of the prison guard. Everything has started to look like a target.

Marty says, "We got matters of life and death in Oakland."

"Everybody does," Mohammed responds. "Everybody wants to go there, and everybody wants to leave."

"Fuck," Marty sneers.

Mohammed regards the two men in the back. The pig-sized eyes of the fat one in the small coveralls are entirely red. The head of the little hairy one is covered by his arms.

"No cursing," Mohammed says.

"You hear that?" Marty reports to Anya.

Anya snuggles obliviously with the kitten, pressing her cheek against the cool glass. She wishes her obligations were finished. If they were, she could ride around with number three son for weeks.

She watches Mohammed's relaxed profile. She listens as he whistles and hums. He smiles mostly to himself, now and then at her. In four years, he is the first American man she has met outside business.

"Who are they?" Anya asks about the photos of children, all shades of brown.

"My babies," Mohammed beams proudly. "Five sons, each named Mohammed after me."

Marty's head returns to Pedro's shoulder.

Mohammed nods in the rearview mirror. "Are they your brothers?"

Anya sputters in disgust. "My brother was beautiful."

"Mine too," Mohammed strokes Anya's hand. "You hungry, little sister?"

"Starving," she whispers.

Mohammed takes out a package of cupcakes from the glove compartment. Anya stuffs the pastry in her mouth. She is hungry, he feeds her. She is cold, he warms her. She is lonely, he fills her. Softly, she begins to cry.

20

Anya has moved over. She is nearly on Mohammed's lap. She sits partly on his one thigh like a child. He calls her Sweet 16 and lets her steer. Marty and Pedro are asleep when they stop at a warehouse between Red Top and El Nido.

"Want to dump them?" Mohammed asks in a whisper. "Over there?"

Anya surveys the empty lot beside the warehouse. Behind the lot is a wrecking yard of junked cars. Behind the stacks of metal parts stands an imposing black mountain of two hundred thousand tires.

"He would kill me," she finally says. "First, he would kill me, then my mother."

Mohammed leans forward to remove a flat ivory sheath from his back pocket. He flips open the single-edge razor.

"We might scare him."

"He don't scare."

"We might kill him."

"He can't die."

"Every man can die. That's how we get to be equal in God's eyes. A liar will say we're born equal. But everybody knows dying is the only thing that makes one man equal to another."

"But he's not a man." Anya turns anxiously to see if Marty is awake. "He's a network."

Mohammed rubs his chin. He knows the menace of networks. That's why he is an independent. That's why he drives only for himself.

That's why he sometimes rents his rig.

He stops at the loading dock on the far side of the warehouse. It's still early. The sun is buried in a gray blanket of clouds. Snow is predicted in the Central Valley by afternoon.

He lightly taps the horn. Anya slides back to her seat.

Two men, bundled in jumpsuits and thick fleece jackets, emerge through a door. Except for their eyes, their faces are covered by ski masks. They look over the driver and the girl.

"I didn't know we were having a party, nigga," one of them grins.

Mohammed grins back. "Nigga, your bad self."

Another pair of men, identically dressed, emerge from the warehouse. They wave their gloved hands at Mohammed.

He nudges Marty and Pedro. "There's a diner down there, and after you eat, we'll be ready to go."

"And Anya?" Marty falters.

"Anya stays here."

Mohammed locks the truck, and he and Anya slip through the warehouse door. It's freezing inside, colder than out. There are no windows. The only source of warmth are the high-powered lights overhead. One of the men hands Anya and Mohammed heavy capes and woolen ski hats.

Stainless steel tables and portable freezers are scattered around the large cavernous room. Hung on one wall and neatly arranged by size are saws, assorted surgical tools. Trough-size sinks and coils of hoses line another wall. Positioned every few feet along the wet floor are drains. The smell of bleach is overwhelming.

Mohammed hurries Anya through an airtight door into a heated room. It too is windowless. However, it's furnished with a couch, table, chairs. There's a hot plate and bathroom.

Anya stumbles towards the shower. Not even after a night of gross sex has she ever felt so filthy.

Mohammed holds up a jumpsuit, similar to the one the men in the warehouse are wearing. Except it's blue. "If you want to throw your clothes away, you can put on this."

The hot water pours over Anya's body. It nearly scalds her. She washes her hair, eyes, breasts, back. Every part of her is soaped and rinsed a dozen times. Someday, she thinks, she will wash the stink of ugly men from her for the last time.

After she is dry, she puts on the jumpsuit. It's big, but the cotton is soft and worn. Underneath, she is naked. She draws on her eyebrows, mink-brown, and wears a shade of pale pink lipstick.

"Sweet 16 all newborn," Mohammed whistles.

Anya glistens. She is pretty and clean except for the bruise on her temple where Marty punched her. She smiles. The elastic movement of her lips across her teeth feels genuine. "Thank you," she says. Her gratitude feels genuine too.

Mohammed sets down coffee, eggs, and toast before her. She eats purposely without speaking. She is clean, and this is the best meal she has ever tasted.

"Where are we?" she finally asks.

"At the edge of heaven and hell," Mohammed answers.

Anya smiles again. She likes his riddles. "Does it have a name?"

"Ararat," he says. "The black mountain behind the warehouse, that's Mount Ararat. That's where Noah landed his ark, and all who were saved, lived. We're there now."

Anya is unfamiliar with the Bible. She has heard stories about Moses and Jesus from Baba, but she has almost forgotten. Ba lit a candle on Sunday and let it burn beside her icon. When she was worried, Ba lit a candle everyday. The police killed her brother because they thought he was Muslim. That's all she knows about religion.

"There was a flood?" Anya asks.

"A great flood drowned the entire earth. It drowned all evil, and only Noah and his family were saved."

One of the men from the warehouse knocks at the door. A rush of cold air enters with him. His ski mask is lifted, and you can see his breath when he speaks.

"Loaded and ready to go," he announces.

Mohammed looks up, "And the others?"

The man nods. "They're back."

"Keep them outside. We'll be ready in a minute."

"You taking them with you?"

Mohammed nods.

"You think that's smart?"

"Smart got nothing to do with it. It's about my exchange with the universe."

"It ain't smart."

"It's protection. Anna's my lucky girl. Aren't you, Anna?"

"Anya," she says.

"I thought you always tell us your protection comes from the magnetic fields."

"Yeah," Mohammed grins. "The balance of positive and negative, North Pole and South Pole, ying and yang, creation and destruction."

"You crazy, nigga."

Mohammed laughs. "Crazy, no," he turns to Anya. "Fool, yes."

21

Cadaver tissue must be carefully handled. Sterile procedures are required. It is mandatory to refrigerate, better yet freeze, tissue within nineteen hours of harvest. At least, two million operations a year require cadaver tissue; and annual sales generate over a billion dollars. Reformers want to limit harvests to non-diseased cadavers and reduce refrigeration requirements to ten hours.

If the tissue spoils, it can necrose in the area of the transplant. Patients can sicken or die of *clostridium sordelli*, alarming doctors, regulators, and the scores of tissue banks that have conducted business without regulations for years.

Mohammed transports tissue and organs all over California. Sometimes he picks up legitimate shipments from airports and delivers them to medical centers. For that, he uses his own truck. Otherwise, he makes lucrative runs out of two warehouses in the Central Valley that specialize in the prison population.

Some prisoners voluntarily donate their organs. Unless they have AIDS, dead prisoners, dead from murder, execution, or natural causes, offer a wealth of opportunity: kidneys, liver, heart, corneas, cartilage, and epidermis. If they have not indicated donation prior to death, a skilled surgeon can harvest a body with a minimum of evidence. When the body is returned to the family, it is clothed and bagged. It is difficult, nearly impossible, to detect missing organs. Even the scars on a prisoner look normal.

In California, harvests from the prison population are a small, specialized niche. It accounts for no more than a few thousand annual donations. Minuscule compared to production in China where execution is more common and thousands of prisoners a year are involuntarily harvested.

Mohammed's single misgiving arises when a living prisoner sells a piece of himself for money or accelerated parole. He doesn't believe a man should sell himself. He believes the body is a divine temple. He considers it a sin.

However, if a man chooses to defile himself for money, that's his personal business. Mohammed's business is to take the merchandise and fulfill the delivery instructions. Half his payment is made at pickup. After delivery, a check for the other half is deposited into his account.

Inside the enclosed portion of the truck, there is now a new unfamiliar generator hum, and the thermometer inside the cab reads below freezing.

"Got to keep it cold back there." Mohammed turns over the ignition. "It'll warm up in here in a minute."

Mohammed's friends wave from the loading dock.

Anya waves back at the friendly, young Americans. She thinks they look like rock 'n roll musicians.

"Are they hippies?" she asks.

"Love children," Mohammed says and flashes them a peace sign.

The truck swings past the giant rubber mound of Mount Ararat and heads towards Highway 152 west.

"Feeling better?" he directs his question to Marty.

Pedro wags his head like a dog. "Beeter."

"Almost human," Marty sighs and mumbles:

Кто жи л и мыслил, тот не может
В душе не презирать людей

"He talking trash?" Mohammed slams the truck to a halt.

"No, no," Anya murmurs, laying her hand over his. "It's a great Russian poem. You know Russians," she smiles and squeezes his fingers. "They only love two things, vodka and poetry. The poet's great-grandfather was black like you. He served in the court of Peter the Great. Ask Marty."

"I serve no man," Mohammed declares.

"From Abyssinia," Marty says.

"They don't love their beautiful Russian women?" Mohammed strokes Anya's pearly neck.

"That's all Russian men are good for. Right, Marty? He's got lines of Pushkin tattooed on his back. Right, Marty?"

"Tell him to talk it in English."

"You hear that, Marty?"

"It ain't so good in English." However, he complies:

> *He who has lived and thought can never*
> *Look on mankind without disdain...*
>
> *He who has felt is haunted ever*
> *By days that will not come again....*

Mohammed is appeased, especially by the feeling of his cold fingers on Anya's warm neck.

"What you put back there?" Marty taps the partition of the cab. His fingers nearly stick to the icy metal.

"Meat to market," Mohammed's laugh ripples. "Got to keep it cold."

"Anya tell you she went on health diet? She don't fucking eat meat no more."

"No cursing, Marty," Mohammed shouts. "Curse again, and I'll sit you down on the side of the highway over there." He points to the desolate crossroads of Highway 152 and I-5. "Somebody might come along to take you to Oakland, but I wouldn't count on it. They don't like hitchhikers out here unless a Mexican brother takes pity on you. You Mexican, ain't you?"

Pedro doesn't respond until Marty slaps him on the head. "He asking you question, stupid."

"Yes," Pedro stutters, "Mexican."

"Up from field to house nigger," Mohammed observes.

"I am Mexican," Pedro attempts to enunciate.

"He doesn't know English good," Anya says with a trace of sympathy. "He just got here a couple of months ago. Where's that place you come from?" Her sympathy expands. She turns to Pedro. "Jalisco?"

For the first time since they met, she smiles at him. She looks directly into his small black eyes and recognizes something familiar. It's a discomforting surprise. "He doesn't know how to take care of himself yet."

Pedro begins to shake. He doesn't like questions. He suspects they will lead to something bad. He has no passport or immigration papers. His driver's license is forged. He has little money.

"You like him?" Mohammed asks.

Anya examines Pedro's hairy head, the tendrils of hair that show in his nostrils and ears, his skinny, hairy fingers and arms. His humanity is a terrifying jolt.

"They call him Tarantula," she muses.

"That's bad," Mohammed says. "That's bad luck. One of them bite you and if you ain't dead quick, you get real real sick."

"They call him that because he's little and hairy and curls up like he's got eight legs. I don't like him. When I look at him, it makes my skin crawl."

"Then I don't like him either."

On the ramp going down to I-5, Mohammed pulls along the shoulder. He leans across Anya and opens the cab door.

"Please get out," he says politely.

Marty restrains himself. "Not good idea." He pats the pocket of his coveralls where his SIG is tucked away. "My leg bum. My head hurt. I die if I get out."

"Nobody talking to you, Poet. If Sweet 16 don't like Spider Man, I don't like him either. If she says the word, you go out too."

"No, he stays." Anya swells with a bit of power.

"He ain't your husband, is he?"

"Not exactly," she confesses. "But we're together."

Marty grimaces. At least, he can still count on Anya's good judgment.

"Your boyfriend then?" Incredulously, he eyes the lumpy man on the backseat.

"We have an agreement," she confides and affectionately rubs Mohammed's thigh. "Like a contract."

"I know about contracts. My brother had his wife killed when she tried to leave."

"She can leave," Marty cries out. "Did she tell you I won't let her leave?"

A shiver runs down Anya's spine. She knows Marty's excitability. It's rare but lethal. "No Marty, you heard what I told him. I told him we have an arrangement. It's a business arrangement."

"That's correct," Marty says quietly, nearly heartsick. He's unsure which is worse: joining Pedro on the side of the road or witnessing Anya's free and affectionate displays towards a stranger.

Pedro climbs out of the truck. Mohammed hands him a ski hat, a baggy sweater, a plastic bag, and a packet of donuts.

"Give him some money," he orders Marty.

Marty fishes out a couple of hundreds from the attaché case. "*Terminado*," he gestures to Pedro.

Pedro shakes his bewildered head. He watches as the truck disappears along the interstate.

"I always keep my word," Anya speaks with a twinge of pride. After almost four years of total dispossession, at least she can say she has kept her word. "In business, it is required," she adds. In fact, this is the only source of pride she has.

"So if you promise me something, you keep it too?" Mohammed teases, touching her row of crooked teeth. They look like a picket fence.

"Maybe," she flirts.

"You better or I won't take you to Oakland."

"What kind of promise?" She teases in return.

Marty massages the trigger of the SIG.

> *It's fun with witty taunts and sallies*
> *To madden an unwary foe,*
> *It's fun to watch him as he rallies*
> *To gore you like a buffalo,...*

Still more delightful to conspire
An honest grave for him to fill,
And at fastidious interval
At his pale brow to aim and fire.
To send him to his fathers, though,
Is poorer fun, I'll have you know.

The land rolls away on either side of the rolling highway as they steadily move north.

22

At the juncture of I-5 and I-580, traffic is stopped. There's a long line of cars, buses, trucks. It's a roadblock. It takes Mohammed an hour to reach the highway patrol. They want to see identification. They don't say why. They say routine, but there's nothing in the routine of I-5 that would ever warrant full closure. Maybe a car chase. Maybe a toxic chemical spill.

Mohammed is calm. He is cool. He has a mind that doesn't panic or react until it has to. He's not an alarmist. He's a rationalist. Rationally, there is no way anyone could know the contents of his truck.

"You two ain't fugitives?" he asks Anya.

"What's that mean?"

"Running away?"

Anya laughs girlishly. "I've been running away since I was a baby. Not such a good idea, it turns out."

At the roadblock, Mohammed shows his driver's license. They type the number into their computer. Marty shows two passports, both from Moldova, one for Oleg Besin and the other for Masha Molofeeva with their photographs. Anya looks much younger. The photograph was taken the day she arrived in the States.

They puzzle over the passports. "Where is this place?" they ask, looking closely at the two foreigners.

"Near Black Sea," Marty answers. "Next to Ukraine."

"Is it the same as Russia?" one patrolman asks another. They don't know.

"Soviet yes, Russia no," Marty sounds reassuring. "Soviet kaput now."

"Where you going?" they inquire.

"Isn't this a free country?" Mohammed challenges.

The patrolmen confer whether to hold the truck.

"Oakland, sir," Marty responds officiously. "We have invitation to visit Mayor of Oakland. We crime specialists from Moldova." He produces a paper that appears to support this mission.

The patrolmen read the letter carefully and wave the truck through.

"What they want?" Mohammed ponders. He fiddles with the radio to try to catch the news. "Terrorists," he concludes.

"Probably practice," Marty says. "Sometimes they practice in Los Angeles. No terrorists, just practice."

Signs suggest Oakland is not very far. Instead of north on I-5, they are now traveling west. It is the first time in a long time, forever it seems, that Anya has been fully awake, neither drugged nor depressed, riding through the American countryside.

The hills are green from the winter rains and dotted with bright yellow sour grass. The sun is warm, opaque, and enveloped with haze.

Anya devours the hillsides of meadows and blossoming plum trees. "How beautiful," she effuses.

"Shut up," Marty mumbles.

"But isn't it beautiful?"

Mohammed smiles at Anya. "A real nature girl," he says.

"A sun-worshiper," she confirms.

Once they top the Altamont pass, Mohammed reports that Oakland is less than an hour away. The eastern slopes of the pass are strewn with windmills that vary in shape, orientation, and blade. Some blades are bowed, some crossed. Some turn, and some are motionless. Hundreds dot the Altamont hills, suggesting that technology is simple, ingenious, benign.

Mohammed and Anya sit closely together. She tells him a beautiful thing about her childhood. She tells him how the smell of hay in the *senoval* is always inside her.

"It's the smell of love," she laughs flirtatiously.

Mohammed makes promises. He says he's a man of his word. He promises to see her once her business arrangement is complete. He promises to take her to an elegant dinner on the San Francisco Bay. "On a boat," he says. He promises never to forget her. Every time he makes a promise, he squeezes Anya's hand.

"Better tell him you maybe gone to Atlanta," Marty interrupts. "Before he promises marry you."

"Shut up, Marty," Anya retorts. "I'm staying in Oakland."

"Whatever Mr. Kupkin says. We take orders from higher power too," Marty adds.

The mention of Mr. Kupkin's name evokes an air of reverence and dread. Anya thinks of him as master puppeteer. It is Mr. Kupkin who owns her.

"As long as Cupcake's not your boyfriend," Mohammed exaggerates a pout.

"Boyfriend?" Marty cries out. "She never even fucked him. He don't allow management, top-down, fucking girls. It's First Commandment."

Mohammed raises his fist, turns half-way in his seat, and shoves it into Marty's chest. "You mind your ugly mouth," he says. "I can put you out right here. They got laws in this country against talking shit."

Anya is flattered. She knows Marty is jealous. She knows he's upset because she will soon be leaving.

As for Mohammed, although he is dark-skinned and middle-aged, he reminds her of a young Greek who once stayed in her town. They have the same almond-shaped eyes and shining teeth. For a couple of months, the Greek was her boyfriend. Whenever she remembers him, she thinks he was the best boyfriend she ever had. Like Mohammed, he was polite. He was gentle. He left her to go to Kosovo to help refugees and was killed by a land mine. When she wants to make herself very sad, she cries over him.

Anya likes Mohammed's old-fashioned manners. But most of all, she likes that he orders Marty around.

Marty says American blacks are animals, and Chinese disgust him. He barely tolerates Mexicans and Jews. Although he cherishes Ethiopians because of Pushkin's great-grandfather, basically he only loves Russians. That's what he is so that's what he loves. Everyone else is stupid, except Chinese and Jews who are greedy and sly. Everyone else is a problem or an obstacle. Either he has to get around them or use them. That's what good about Mexicans, he says. They're easy to use, but blacks aren't easy. Marty says they're over-liberated.

At I-680 Mohammed steers the truck north towards Sacramento.

"Oakland that way," Marty points frantically to the disappearing sign.

"Don't have a cardiac, man," Mohammed says cooly. "All roads lead to Oakland."

"We want straight road," Marty protests.

"Too much traffic that way."

Soon signs for Oakland appear again. They pass Lafayette, Moraga, Orinda, names Anya will ever-after associate with liberty. She can feel her stomach quiver.

Traffic slows at the Caldicott tunnel, a feat of engineering that burrows under the range of hills that divides the San Francisco Bay from valleys and more hills. And cities from suburbs too.

Anya reads the restrictions: *No explosives, flammables, liquified petroleum gas, or poisonous gas in tank truck, trailer, or semitrailer except from 3 am to 5 am.*

Mohammed tells her there was a fire years ago inside the tunnel when an oil tanker blew up and seven people were killed.

As they enter the tunnel, the highway narrows to two lanes. As a precaution, Mohammed turns on his lights. At the far end, when they emerge from the dark tube, a vista of sunny blue sky and sparkling blue water erupts before them. The layers of hazy clouds have vanished. It's as if the world has been one thing before the tunnel and after it, it's entirely something else. A magical destination. Girders from the spans of bridges flash, and the skyline of San Francisco sparkles in the distance.

A cry stalls in Anya's throat. She has nearly reached the end, she thinks. It's the end of the continent, the end of the country, and nearly the end of her voyage.

A single siren interrupts her reverie. It is rushing at them from behind. Sirens always frighten her.

Marty cranes his neck to peer out the truck's side mirror. He can't recall such a terrible day of misjudgments, one after another. He groans aloud. He doesn't like to make messes for Mr. Kupkin. He likes to do everything right.

As the siren approaches, Mohammed slows and steers to the right. He expects the CHP to pass, but instead the car and its flashing cherry-top light cruise alongside the cab.

Through a loudspeaker, the command reverberates, "Pull over. Pull over now…now…now."

Mohammed shrugs. He lifts his hands off the wheel. "What did I do, man?" He mouths the words to the officer on the passenger side.

An arm extends from the window and motions him to the side of the road as the loudspeaker continues to command, "Pull over now… now…now."

"Fuck," Marty exhales.

This time Mohammed does not reprimand him. However, he is perfectly calm. He touches his thumb to his lips and transfers the kiss to the Buddha and the small face of Bob Marley. He squeezes Anya's hand with reassurance. He brakes the vehicle and waves to the cops.

"It's harassment," he tells her. "You ever hear of DWB?"

As the CHP slows down to park, a scene, also from a movie Mohammed can't quite remember, possesses him. He floors the accelerator and tears down the highway, lurching and swerving past the exit to Berkeley.

"He kill us." Marty yanks Anya's hair. "He kill us now."

The truck cuts to the right on the shoulder and jams up the steeply banked ramp to Highway 13. Anya is tossed towards the passenger door. She grabs the overhead strap and tucks the kitten under the seat.

"Stop him, Anya," Marty yells.

"Stop," she orders weakly. She can't hear her voice over the other noises.

Mohammed turns and gives her a wild-eyed look. He clutches his peyote feather in one hand and steers the careening vehicle with the other.

"Stop! You crazy son of bitch!" Marty screams, pushing the end of his gun into Mohammed's ear.

Mohammed's hands slip from the wheel as the truck spins over the incline. Several tons of metal roll over, land right side up, and crash through a stand of eucalyptus trees.

Anya is thrown from the truck. She feels herself suspended in slow motion. The broad, smiling faces of her grandmother, her brother, the handsome Greek youth fill the airy space between the trees. She bounces once and lands on a mound of eucalyptus leaves.

After some minutes, the pungent camphor smell revives her. She opens first one eye, then two. She wiggles her fingers, her toes. They move with familiarity. She makes an effort to lift her torso, but a heavy painful weight prevents her.

Lying beside her on the ground are several frosty globules. They are purplish brown, the color of a certain mushroom Ba used to gather. One glob resembles unwashed calf's liver. Another a kidney. A third is an eyeball that is white, red, and blue.

Anya wonders if they belong to her. She touches her abdomen but feels no holes or blood.

The truck has stopped some yards ahead. Its back doors are wide open. Neither Marty nor Mohammed are in view. The horn and sirens are silent. She hears only the shouts of the two policemen who have tumbled by foot down the bank behind them.

23

Mr. Kupkin has brought the new girl to Oakland himself. She behaved well on the journey only because he told her they were going back home.

However, Tuzla is not stupid or blind. As soon as they arrive in California, she resumes her attacks. She tries to bite him as they deboard the plane.

In way of explanation, Kupkin shows airport security a medical license and explains that the traumatized woman is under his care. They help get her into handcuffs and a wheelchair and escort them to a waiting area where Kupkin injects her with a sedative. Once she is subdued, they help him get her outside to a waiting limousine.

Tuzla is one of Kupkin's latest shipment of girls from Bosnia. Unlike the half-dozen others, she has been trouble ever since she arrived. It's not the typical trouble that is quiet and mournful. Or angry brooding. Tuzla is a wildcat. She likes to tear, scratch, bite.

Kupkin likes her feisty nature. He likes a rebel. He respects a fighter. He even welcomes a little challenge. But he recognizes that Tuzla's excess energy is only an asset if it can be harnessed. So far, what could be used to her advantage and converted into a high-paid attraction, has persisted as a problem.

Normally, after a week or two of orientation, new team members acquiesce. The girls are treated respectfully as part of an elite. The orientation is designed to soften them with shopping consultations, hair stylists, pedicures, health spas. They're instructed in policies that apply to sick leave, accounting procedures, and death benefits for their families. Ultimately, they accept the terms of the contract. They accept the fact they have no choice.

Tuzla has consistently refused to calm down. She throws fits and food. She shreds clothes. She kicks furniture and televisions. She's absolutely enraged.

Kupkin found Tuzla in Sarajevo, begging on the street. He watched her dance for hours to the same Michael Jackson tape near one of the bombed-out parks. They were mesmerizing, undulating dances. When Kupkin first approached her, he gave her a portable CD player and all his discs.

Not only does Tuzla dance well, but she is truly beautiful. In fact, she is the most beautiful girl he has ever recruited. He doesn't understand why someone didn't marry her. Or offer her a job as a model. But perhaps she is unbalanced. Perhaps she's mentally ill. Perhaps the war made her crazy.

Nonetheless, she is breathtaking to behold. More than beautiful, she is an original. He has never seen her likeness.

Kupkin plans to use Tuzla in his clubs. He has promised she can dance, and he sincerely means it. To dance in America is her greatest desire. But she refuses to strip or fuck. She is fundamentally against coercion. Over and over, he has explained the terms of the contract, but still she refuses.

To date, the success of Kupkin's girls has been built on strict equality. He shows no favoritism. He expects his managers to show none either. If a girl goes beyond expectations like Anya, he may occasionally give her a strand of pearls or an extra day off. He also made an exception with Cerise. Because she was so young and frail, he let her skip the lap-dancing circuit. But these instances are rare.

Peer pressure usually speeds adaptation. In special cases, advice from a veteran goes a long way. But Tuzla is baffling. She has no interest in advice or temptations. She says she prefers to go home to ruins. She says she'd rather be a beggar than a slave.

Slave is a forbidden word in Kupkin's domain.

"There are no slaves here," he declares. "Debtors yes, slaves no."

This distinction means a lot to him. It's not a barbaric operation.

It's not a sweatshop lacking rules and regulations. He wants it understood that the girls are under contract for a specified amount of money and time. It's what he calls a "civilized opportunity." He takes excellent care of his employees, and they receive papers and cash when they leave. The more they work, the sooner they are free to go. It's a simple mathematical formula, and the girls are all sufficiently educated to understand the equation.

Like most immigrants, Kupkin's beginnings were humble. Although he has an innate knack for hustling, more importantly he is a keen observer. He carefully observes, then carefully makes his move. His interest in money is held in check by prudence. He is neither foolish nor rash.

The girls came along as a side-line after he started making regular trips to Russia to buy icons. In Moscow he was accosted by young, pretty girls who offered themselves to him for a meal. Many girls. He had no interest in the sex, but he was glad to treat them to dinner. He observed that most were not degenerate, only desperate to leave Russia. It penciled out on paper to be worth the risk.

Kupkin has recently turned sixty. He lives with his wife of thirty-five years in a large columned house near Buckhead, Atlanta's best suburb. He considers it a shame that he has no children. He plays tennis three times a week and when in town, keeps up a hectic social calendar. He is on the board of several charities and has a special interest in health issues related to women.

Small and slender, Kupkin's carriage is utterly erect. It is topped by a sculpted intelligent head and a face distinguished by a long sloping nose and pale blue eyes. His hair is dyed black and stylishly cropped. His suits are custom-made in Hong Kong, his shoes are English, his ties Italian silk. His business cards are expensively engraved:

Jean-Paul Kupkin
J.P.K. International
IMPORT & TRADE

In addition to the girls and Russian Orthodox icons, he also deals in rustic furniture from the countryside of the Ukraine, Slovakia, and Czech Republic. He has extensive real-estate holdings and owns buildings in other cities across the country: Baltimore, Charlotte, Houston, Denver, Los Angeles, Oakland, Seattle.

All the girls begin their tour in Atlanta. Atlanta is central head-quarters for J.P.K. International. The five-storey brick building on West Peachtree Street was originally constructed as a residence hotel. Most of the first floor is comprised of open offices, devoted to sales, communications, customer service, data collection, and human resources for the three major J.P.K. divisions: religious artifacts, antique furnishings, and party management.

To date, forty girls have passed through orientation. Nine have worked their way out of the system after a production period of five years. Two have died.

The girls are scattered in units of six to eight plus two-person management teams across the country. They are posted at sites where they stay one to three months. Then, they are rotated out of the area to another site to minimize client attachments and keep the supply of girls fresh.

This latest enterprise has transformed Kupkin from rich to extremely wealthy. However, it is no exaggeration to say the girls' welfare has given his life meaning. They are infinitely more interest-ing than either icons or furniture, despite their troubles. And they constantly inspire him to perform the versatile tasks of counselor, confessor, patron, and provider.

24

Kupkin's operation in Oakland has not officially begun. Renovations on the newly acquired building by Lake Merritt are still underway.

When he and Tuzla arrive, there is no one around. The workmen have taken off for lunch. Marty and Anya are still en route from Los Angeles.

The hired driver helps move Tuzla to a bedroom on the second floor overlooking the lake. She is sleeping fitfully, but at least she is sleeping.

Kupkin is impatient for Marty to arrive. The trip across country with Tuzla has worn him out. He is nervous and tired. He does not want to be alone when she wakes up. He is counting on Marty and Anya to take charge.

Kupkin tries Marty's cell phone. There is no answer, only an OUT OF SERVICE reply. The LA office informs him that Marty left with Pedro and Anya before midnight and expected to arrive in Oakland for a morning meeting with the construction crew. However, the foreman of the crew knows nothing. Neither does Kupkin's office in Atlanta. Marty has left no message anywhere, even on Kupkin's restricted private number at home.

Except for gambling, Marty is a reliable and punctual employee. The only distraction Kupkin can conceive is an impulsive detour to Las Vegas. Kupkin suspects Marty made Pedro drive them to Nevada so he could spend a few quick hours at the tables before heading into Oakland.

"Fucking rat," Kupkin mutters.

He himself dials the registration desks of the Bellagio, Cesar's Palace, and Mandalay Bay. He instructs the Atlanta office to try other hotels. There is no one registered under Marty or his aliases.

Every few minutes, Kupkin checks his watch. He calls Los Angeles again. He orders an assistant manager to get on a plane to Oakland and bring along one of the veteran girls.

Tuzla opens and closes one eye. She is groggy. Her eyelids feel like lead. Her brain is stuffed with wadding. The bridge of her nose is tight. Her ears ring. She tries to turn her head. She wonders if she is shackled. She lifts a wrist off the bedspread. She can't feel any rope or wire. She opens her other eye. Her tormentor stands nearby. In the far, far distance she can hear him talking on the phone. He is by the window. His jacket is folded on the back of a chair. She can faintly make out a sour expression on his face. He looks as if he has sucked a lime. She prefers it when he's upset. She hates him most when he smiles.

"Where are we?" she mumbles.

"They better fucking get here soon," he replies.

"Who?"

"Raise voice and I stick you," he threatens.

Tuzla can manage nothing fierce in return. She is limp. Her brain most of all. Parts of her are disconnected from each other. She can't feel herself whole. She pulls the covers to her chin and rolls over.

Kupkin calls Atlanta again. It's the fifth time in a half-hour. No one has heard from Marty. He puts his entire staff on alert. He orders someone to check all California hospitals. He orders a manager in Houston to fly to Las Vegas. He redials Marty's cell phone.

"Pointless," Kupkin says.

Tuzla is sleepy but doesn't want to sleep. Under the covers, she pinches herself trying to wake up.

She senses that something has not gone well. She has never seen Kupkin agitated. Even when they have physically struggled, he maintains an impenetrable veneer. Now she can see where the veneer has cracked. He paces. He is distraught. He picks up the phone, puts it down. He turns on and off the television. He curses to himself in Russian.

"Either way, he's dead man," Kupkin finally says.

Tuzla drifts. A square pane of sunlight shines directly on her face. Like Anya, she too worships the sun. The day itself is freedom. But she fears the night. The night unhinges her. Kupkin's presence unhinges her too. He makes her want to rip his suit and tear the gold chain from his neck. She wants to wrap his tie around his throat and watch his tongue explode. She wants to see him shriveled, cold, naked. She wants to take a knife and carve into the soft flesh of his underarm. She wants to carve the names of her mother, father, brothers, sister.

So far he has managed to stop her from doing these things. Whenever she loses control, he sticks her. He takes his needle and sticks her. The liquid in the needle makes her disappear.

Tuzla hates disappearing. She tells herself that tonight she will stay composed. She will not tear at him. She will do the intelligent thing. She will think instead of act. She will use her will-power. She will lie still and listen.

A few minutes pass. Tuzla can feel the strength of will returning to her limbs. Will flows into her like fresh blood as the drug flows out. The parts reassemble into a whole unit. It's as if she has been reborn. The pressure lifts from her nose and ears. The fuzziness leaves her brain. She squeezes her fists and curls her feet. She flexes her legs. She rotates her neck and arches her spine.

Then, in one suspended airborne movement, Tuzla leaps from the bed and pounces onto Kupkin's back. Her weight propels them forward towards the window where Kupkin's hands manage to block the fall and keep the glass from breaking.

The noise, however, attracts one of the workmen. From the street he sees Kupkin's face pressed to the glass and a small figure clutching his back.

"Get her onto bed," Kupkin commands as three workmen storm the door. They drag the girl over to the bed. She is small but shockingly strong.

Kupkin smoothes his shirt and retucks it into his pants. He curses Marty again.

"He wants me to fuck him," the girl screams in a jumble of languages. "He makes me fuck him."

The workmen are uneasy. They do not know what they're supposed to do.

Kupkin adjusts his face. Once again his countenance is focused, assured.

"I am medical doctor. Girl is patient under my care." He touches his temple to indicate something is wrong with her mind. "The war in Bosnia," he says with grave concern. "Raped many times in the war."

Tuzla's screams have broken down into large sobs. "I want to die," she sobs. "Let me die, die, die."

"I brought her here for special treatment," Kupkin continues.

"Kill me," Tuzla cries.

"There is treatment center here," he explains. "Center that help victims of war. They help like her who have been tortured and raped."

"Then what should we do?" one of the bewildered workmen asks. He has not heard of Bosnia.

"This evening we have appointment here," Kupkin says. He checks his watch. "Specialist coming to examine her. He knows what to do."

25

By early evening, some of the pieces are sorted out. Tuzla is again sedated and securely tied down. The team from Los Angeles has arrived. Marty and Anya have been located at Highland Hospital in Oakland. Marty is in a coma with multiple fractures in his right arm and leg, a ruptured spleen, and collapsed lung. Anya is in shock with a broken rib and abrasions. No one knows the whereabouts of the van or Pedro. The police have charged Mohammed McRae of Richmond, California, driver of the truck, with a range of crimes. He is in critical condition. As of yet, there are no charges against Anya and Marty. Kupkin is waiting for more information before he identifies them as J.P.K. employees.

Kupkin has left the apartment by the lake and checked into the Claremont Hotel, an enormous rock and white stucco structure originally built in 1915 with a large central tower, a veranda, spectacular views, and acres of garden. After a shot of single-malt scotch and excellent New York strip, he's feeling more optimistic. He's looking forward to a morning swim in the heated hotel pool and a sauna to resolve the small irritation of Tuzla's attack.

The irritation of Tuzla herself, however, is a great deal bigger. He's almost convinced she's irremediable. He had hopes Anya could pitch in, but perhaps it's a hopeless case after all. No matter about her beauty and talent. Or his personal investment in airfare and clothing. His business is not a charity. It's a business. Every good businessman knows when to cut his losses.

Kupkin evaluates the situation. Marty's health is an unknown. At best, he will require surgery and long weeks of physical therapy. Anya, although still indisposed, should be available in a day or two. He can afford to wait for Anya.

"Tuzla," he utters the name like a synonym for devil. He rubs the sore spots on his neck. He thinks she intended to push him out the window. She must have wanted to kill him. He is surprised. He has never had anyone try to kill him. And with her own hands? She must have seen the bars on the window and tried to push him anyway. It doesn't make sense. But if she's genuinely crazy, why should it make sense?

It bothers Kupkin that she wanted to kill him. It bothers him she repays his generosity with attempted murder after he picked her off the street, no less from the gutter. That makes no sense either.

So far he has been lucky with his girls. Out of forty, this is the first to deliberately, persistently cause trouble. There have been crying fits, homesickness, cat fights. There have been two unfortunate deaths in the bed. Plus three cases of HIV. Nevertheless, he has been lucky. Until now, he has had no bona fide lunatics.

Kupkin sits at the picture window of the hotel watching the lights. Far below, the lights twinkle all around. Except for the large, dark patch of water and large, dark patch of sky, there are lights everywhere. His bedroom is unremarkable, but the vast white hotel resembles a fairyland. The illuminated paths of the gardens, luscious even in winter, meander and connect to the tennis courts and turquoise pool.

Kupkin ruminates. If Tuzla proves absolutely hopeless, he must realistically consider alternatives. He can't fire her. Or turn her loose. Or give her identity papers, a few dollars, and wish her luck.

He can keep her unconscious. That might have an appeal for an elite group of squeamish necrophiliacs. She could be pronounced either half-dead or half-alive, depending on a client's proclivity. Experience has proven there are a sufficiently large number of men who want to fuck a truly beautiful woman in any condition. That could potentially be lucrative.

But whether Tuzla is comatose or awake, in her current state she would require full-time supervision. She would have to be treated like an invalid. She would have to be fed, bathed, and dressed. She would have to be constantly watched, whether sleeping or fucking. Beauty aside, it would be hard to justify that kind of expense.

Another possibility occurs to him. The next time Tuzla acts up, he can call the police. When they arrive, he can tell them she's a stranger who attacked him. He can file a complaint and have her prosecuted for assault, breaking-and-entering, theft, attempted murder, etc.

Here again, there's an obvious drawback. He doesn't want the obligation or inconvenience of court appearances in California. That could prove a bigger headache and expense than a sedated Tuzla.

Better yet, he can drop her outside the I.C.E. offices in San Francisco. If she thinks he's a nightmare, wait until she encounters the United States government. They will jail her for months or years. They will move her from prison to prison. They will treat her as a criminal whether she has been charged, tried, convicted, or not. She will get buried in their swamp, and once they finally figure out where she belongs, they will deport her back to Bosnia.

It gives Kupkin satisfaction to imagine her in prison, but this too is a risk. There could always be the chance interpreter, the concerned do-gooder, the sympathetic fellow prisoner who helps her piece a story together. With a story comes the remote possibility that some nosey or eager investigator could eventually find him. Or Amnesty International or a women's rights organization get involved.

As a last resort, Kupkin can have someone kill her. He shudders, although it is the cleanest, most practical solution. Not only does it have to be carefully planned, it has to remain a secret.

If Marty comes out of his coma, he is the obvious choice. He has openly expressed an interest. Ever since he got the SIG, he takes it with him everywhere. He prefers to drive instead of fly so he can carry it at all times. He goes to shooting ranges. He shows it off. With good humor, he often asks Kupkin if there isn't someone he can whack.

Kupkin doesn't like that Marty is trigger-happy. He doesn't like Marty to ask. He considers it indiscreet. He has seen that Marty has a tendency to gloat. He's the sort of Russian who brags on himself by quoting long tracts of Pushkin. He says in prison, he had only one book, *Eugene Onegin*, and to pass the time, he memorized it. He likes to show off his tattoos where Pushkin is quoted.

Kupkin thinks Marty not only gloats but tries to win everyone's sympathy. He wants to impress the girls that his life is as hard as theirs. Kupkin thinks a sentimentalist doesn't make a very good killer. To be a killer, you have to care more about the present than the past.

Anyway, Kupkin doesn't approve of Marty's violent tendencies. He is proud his fortune has been built with so little violence. He likes to say his pleasures are passive. He appreciates antiques, icons, and girls.

He does not like to consider murder. But he argues to himself, Tuzla actually tried to murder him. Is killing her *within reason* or not? That's the litmus test for Kupkin's decisions, and the weighty words, *within reason*, carry the entire philosophy of the company.

Kupkin feels for the teeth marks on the back of his neck. In this case, he thinks he can easily justify self-defense.

26

Anya dreams of an eyeball. In its center is a circle. The circle is tinted blue and clear like the Caribbean. She peers through the crystalline center and spies the center of another identical but slightly smaller eyeball. Circumscribing the center are thin bands of different colors and around the bands is white jelly. The eye is divided by four red arrows that intersect at the center and the entire sphere surrounded by a golden nimbus. While the center remains perfectly still, the aqueous humor pulses inward as if punched from its other side.

In the dream, Anya plucks the eyeball out of its aura. It slides easily into her palm like the yoke of a raw egg. While she holds it, the pulsing of the white jelly stops.

Now when Anya looks into the center, instead of another eye she sees veins, blood, and cartilage magnified inside her palm. She moves the eyeball to her arm, and the same phenomenon occurs. Instead of a clear, empty center, she can see inside her own body.

She tries again. She puts the eyeball on her chest. But in its center instead of her heart, there is a black, spindly spider wiggling in a little spider dance.

Anya screams. She tries to brush the eyeball or spider, she is not sure which, away from her. However, its underside has created a terrible suction which cannot be torn away. She pulls at the suction cup. Finally, she can feel it loosening. Finally, it gives way.

She flings it from her as far as possible. She closes her eyes after this great effort, but when she opens them again, there are more eyeballs, hundreds in all sizes, all with clear centers.

She tries to rise, but her torso is strapped in a bed. The eyeballs are gone. She is surrounded by the white walls of a small room. Beside the bed several plastic bags hang connected to tubes, all of them going into her arm. By the bed is a television suspended from the wall and next to the pillow, a buzzer. There is no clock. The blinds of the window are shut.

She tries the buzzer. A distant voice responds. It sounds unfriendly.

Anya attempts to speak, but her mouth is extremely dry. Her tongue sticks to her palate.

"Water," Anya manages.

"Turn to the right," the voice instructs.

Anya revolves her head. On a stand within reaching distance is a plastic cup with a straw.

"Thank you," she whispers gratefully.

"Good night," the distant voice signs off abruptly.

Next to the cup is a plate covered by a metal dome. Anya lifts the dome. Beside a piece of fried chicken is a spoonful of cold potatoes and a few cooked carrots. Anya grabs the dinner roll and smears it with a tab of margarine. She devours it. She is starving. She could eat a dozen rolls.

She tries again to rise. Not only is she strapped in, but a complex of tubes encircle her. Some connect to the plastic bags, others to suction tabs on her chest and head. One tube dangles pointlessly where she has torn the suction tab off.

Anya presses the buzzer again. There is no answer. She waits a few seconds.

"She's on the floor," the disembodied voice reports.

"Can I have another roll?" Anya meekly asks.

"She'll be in shortly." Followed by what is already a familiar and abrupt disconnection.

Shortly is correct. Instantly, a tiny woman in a pink uniform enters the room. She slips on a pair of latex gloves from a box by the door.

"My name is Nancy. I'm your nurse for the night." She states with disinterest. "Awake?"

"I guess so."

"How do you feel?"

"Hungry," Anya responds.

The nurse sticks a thermometer under Anya's tongue, checks the level of fluids, picks up the suction tab from the floor, and tosses it into the garbage.

"You can't tear off your tabs," she scolds, taking out the thermometer and proceeding with the blood pressure.

"I was dreaming," Anya explains.

"Nightmare is more like it," the nurse smiles without parting her lips. "When patients start tearing things off, it usually means nightmare. Am I right?"

"Where am I?"

"Where do you think?" The nurse's smile widens, and Anya can see braces across the front of her teeth. Like the rest of her, the teeth are abnormally small.

In the distance are sirens. One approaches. It gets louder and louder until it roars. No matter where she is, there are sirens. Anya thinks a siren is a clarion call to hell.

"I mean, is this a city?" she asks.

The nurse pulls up her gloves. Her movements are quick and jerky. She undoes Anya's flimsy hospital gown and pokes a finger into her diaper. Then, she reties the gown and tucks the sheet and blanket tightly around her body.

"You're in Oakland, California."

Anya is cheered. "We made it to Oakland," she says.

The nurse checks the chart. There is little patient information. She came in without identification. No name, no age, no address, no next of kin. Only time of ER admission, a packet of chest X-rays, diagnosis, notations on temperature, and blood pressure.

"Where're you from?" the nurse asks. She herself is from East Timor.

"Kursk." Anya regards the woman to see if there is any sign of recognition.

The nurse's black eyes are tired but bright. Anya sees facets of life in her eyes. On the pocket of her pink uniform is an embroidered tag: NANCY.

"I maybe heard of it before. Over by Stockton maybe. You had a bad accident. You remember that?"

Anya nods. She remembers flying off a hill. She remembers the smiling faces of Ba and her brother. And a sharp odor. Maybe camphor. She remembers the back doors of the truck, swinging back and forth as if someone had just forced them open although no one was in sight.

Anya searches for other memories. A number of slimy globs encircle her like candles around the dead. White globs with colored bands, red arrows, and clear centers like the eyeballs in her dream. She remembers hearing the cop curse when he stopped to pick one up. He threw it down like a snake. Then, he vomited. The smell of vomit and eucalyptus made Anya vomit too.

Unexpectedly, Anya screams.

"You hurting?" Nancy asks, taking her pulse.

Anya does hurt. Her ribs ache whenever she moves. Even when she talks, they hurt. What hurts more than her body is the thought of her little gray kitten. Most likely, it's dead. If not dead, lost. And if dead or hungry or lost, it's her fault. She might as well have murdered it.

"If I give you a painkiller, you'll sleep to morning," Nancy rambles. "You sleep through and dream about Kursk. No nightmares."

"I'm too hungry to sleep," Anya says.

Nancy speedily leaves the room but holds up her dainty brown fingers to indicate she is coming back. She returns with a cup of hot instant soup and packets of crackers. She sits by the bed and spoons the soup into Anya's mouth.

"So where's your family?" Nancy asks.

"Near Kursk."

"All in Kursk. You want to call somebody? And tell them you're here?"

Anya shakes her head.

"You got nobody to call?"

Tears fill Anya's eyes and drop onto her cheek. It has been a long time since her eyes made tears. It's a comforting sensation. Sometimes when she watches the new girls distressed and distraught, she wishes she could cry too.

The nurse hands her a tissue. "You homeless, huh?"

Anya is uncertain how to answer. The tears continue to fall. Her head feels hot. It is hard to think while she is crying.

"That's not my business," Nancy continues. "But you came with no ID. The police will want to know where you and your boyfriend live."

"How is…my boyfriend?" Anya asks uncertainly.

"Now is not the time to upset you."

"I'm already upset," Anya shrugs. "It won't upset me more."

The nurse leans over with a spoonful of soup and whispers, "He's in ICU. He's in a coma."

"Which one?" Anya asks.

Nancy is puzzled.

"The pink one with the beard or the black one?"

The nurse is now confused. She stares at the place on Anya's face where there should be eyebrows. "Which is your boyfriend?"

Anya can't calculate while she's crying. She buries her face in the tissue and continues to snuffle. She can't decide which man to claim. Maybe one of them is dead. Maybe one of them is dying. Maybe one of them is wanted by the law. There's a smart answer, but Anya doesn't know what it is.

"Do they think he'll be all right?"

Nancy leaves but again holds up a finger to indicate she'll speedily return.

Anya recalls another piece of the accident. The police tried to get Mohammed to stop. They waved him to the side of the road. They called through a loudspeaker. They issued commands. They said, "Pull over now…now…now." But Mohammed disobeyed. He accelerated and drove away from the police.

"Badly broken bones," the nurse reports. "Compound fractures, ruptured spleen."

Anya wants to be sure. "You mean the white man or black?"

"Is one of them really your boyfriend?"

Anya says sadly, "I don't know either one."

Nancy takes a seat by the bed. "You hitchhiking or something?"

Anya doesn't respond. The room is silent, blank. Absent is color of almost any kind. She finds the blankness soothing. She feels protected.

"Am I dying?" Anya asks hopefully. The room looks like a tomb for either the living or dead.

The nurse shakes her head. She settles into the chair. It's the middle of the night. There is time to keep the girl company.

"How long can I stay here?" Anya touches the wrinkled cotton gown. It's a protection too. It's the only clothing she now has, and it's a loan. The loose sack is completely devoid of any allure. It reminds Anya of the cheap housecoat her grandmother wore for spring cleaning. Every spring Ba wrapped the bushy end of a broom with a pillowcase and used it to sweep away the cobwebs. She went over the corners and ceilings of the house, even the *senoval*. Anya wonders if she were to die, would Mr. Kupkin ship her body back to Russia?

"A couple of days more," Nancy says. "At least, for observation."

"Observation?" The word is frightening. For the last four years Anya's life and its most intimate aspects have been nothing but an obscene observation.

"In case there's internal bleeding," Nancy explains. "But you are young. The young heal quickly. They forget quickly too. Those are both good things."

Anya sinks into the pillow. "And then?"

"Then you are free to go." Nancy pats Anya's hand.

Anya's emaciated face breaks into a grin. Such a casual off-hand suggestion. She repeats to be sure, "Free to go?"

Nancy appraises the patient. There's a large bruise on her temple. She looks malnourished and abused. She studies the girl's pretty face: the traces of acne, the brilliant slanted eyes, the crooked teeth, the intermittent childlike expressions.

Again, she reviews the chart. At admitting, there were almost no personal belongings. Only a pair of high-heeled shoes were checked into the hospital's depository. The jumpsuit Anya wore at the time of the accident was confiscated by the police.

"You'll need clothing, but we have a service here that can find you something to wear."

Nancy jots down Anya's different sizes for shoes, jeans, bra, shirt, sweater, and coat.

The buzzer rings. The nurse rushes out for a few minutes and rushes back in. In the short interval, Anya's countenance has brightened. She has imagined yet another future. A future of anonymity. A fantasy of nameless wandering.

"What if you are homeless?" Anya wants to know.

"So that is the case?"

"Do they take you to jail?"

Nancy wonders if this girl, injured and stranded, has never been to a city before now.

"No one cares if you're homeless," Nancy admits. She guesses the girl must have run away from home. She must have run to I-5 from Kursk, caught a ride, and gotten into an unfortunate accident.

"They let you live on the street or anywhere?"

"If you break the law, if you urinate in public, if you disobey the police, they put you away. Otherwise, nobody bothers you." Nancy swiftly adds, "But you don't want to be out on the street."

Anya thinks maybe it's possible to live without papers. Maybe she can say her purse and papers were thrown from the truck. She can make up an address and name. If Marty can't corroborate, she can say anything she wants. She tries to move. She wants to leave immediately.

Nancy raises the blinds on the window. From the bed Anya sees a single leafless tree. She has never seen anything as thrilling in her life. A great swell of affection goes to the tree. Tree of life, she remembers Ba saying. That was the name of the tapestry her father brought back from England. "Tree of life," she murmurs.

"The weather is bad, and the streets are dangerous," Nancy says, looking out the window. "You need protection on the street. If you have no money, you have to beg. Unless you find a shelter, you have to search every night for a safe, dry place to sleep."

Nancy watches the girl's face, completely reposed, completely soft. She looks like many other young people. A little troubled, a little raw.

"Can't you go home?" Nancy asks.

The tear ducts swell and overflow again. Anya could call herself a citizen of the world, but unlike Marty, she is not a sentimentalist. She is cruelly realistic. She left behind a bleak life: hunger, unemployment, pointlessness. She is now an immigrant, orphan, illegal alien, and whore.

Anya shakes her head because there is no way to explain.

27

In the morning when Anya opens her eyes, Kupkin is by her side. He is seated in Nancy's chair. He holds the *Wall Street Journal* and a piece of soggy toast from Anya's breakfast tray. His trench coat is folded at the foot of her bed. The cuffs of his woolen trousers and shoes are splattered with dried mud.

Anya shuts her eyes trying to block out the sight of him, but one sob is irrepressible.

"There, there," Kupkin tosses the paper aside and takes Anya's hand. He is fond of her. She has been almost trouble-free.

"How did you find me?" She weeps, peering through the partially closed blinds. The lights in the room are dim. Anya can see that one plate of food has been removed, and another has replaced it. Outside it is stormy. The tree's limbs shake, and a hard rain hammers the window glass.

"Of course, I find you. You don't think I let you rot outside there." He points through the window. "As long as you work for me, I take care of you. That's the deal."

Kupkin lifts the metal dome off the breakfast plate. Scrambled eggs, sausage, toast, apple sauce. Anya motions for him to close the lid again. The sausage makes her gag.

"Where is Nancy?" she asks.

"Who?"

"My nurse, Nancy."

"Shift changed." Kupkin checks his watch, sets it three hours back to Pacific Standard Time. "She left."

"Is she coming back?"

"How should I know? Anyways it don't matter. You won't be here."

"Nancy said I have to stay two days. They have to keep me in for observation."

"I know that." Kupkin breaks off a corner of toast.

Anya cries, "In case there's internal bleeding."

"I made arrangement. They releasing you this afternoon." He pats his breast pocket. "Into care of Dr. Kupkin."

Anya starts to squirm, but the pain in her ribs stops her.

"I can't move. I can't do anything. Who will take care of me?"

Kupkin silences Anya with an omniscient smile and settles back in the chair to resume reading.

"How's Marty?" she interrupts.

"The police took gun and attaché case. He should have thrown them out window, but it's hard to think so fast under circumstance. You two took tremendous crash." Kupkin is impressed anyone survived. "I had to explain nature of our business in order to get papers back."

Kupkin smiles slyly. He is skilled at explanations. In fact, if he had to claim genius at anything, it would fall into the realm of explanations.

Concerning the unusual papers in Marty's attaché case, Kupkin has told the police they are welcome to copies, but as an official in Interpol, he has to retrieve the originals. He has explained that Marty is a member of the international team, investigating forged documents for illegal aliens who originate in Eastern Europe. Kupkin is Marty's boss, and Anya is undercover, acting as one of the imports. Naturally, Kupkin has Interpol identification for all three of them. He has also called Congresswoman Hinkle from Georgia who sits on the advisory board of Kupkin's non-profit, Women vs. AIDS. Hinkle's staff person in Washington has spoken to Oakland's Chief of Police.

The Oakland authorities are not interested in the business of forgery. Their concern over the contents of the attaché case is fueled by its relationship to the contents of cargo on the truck. So far, there does not appear to be a connection. They have informed Kupkin that he can pick up Marty's belongings later in the afternoon.

"What about his condition?"

"They don't know when he wakes up. They don't know anything. I want him transferred out of this hole."

Kupkin sighs loudly and lowers his eyes. Marty is a great loss. Marty is a right-hand man. "It's least I can do. We should all pray. Pray he either recovers or dies because nobody wants to be in between. You know, Anya? You were lucky. It may not look that way, but at least you not lying downstairs like cabbage." Kupkin almost chokes with emotion. His eyes flutter as he continues to speak softly. "And Marty, he loved taking special care of you. You know how he was with you? Always bringing special things for you? I hope you going to pray for him."

Anya closes her eyes. The only prayer she can think of is that Marty die, go straight to hell, and stinking rot there forever. She hopes there's a God to answer her prayer.

After a moment of silence has passed, Anya asks. "What about the driver?"

Kupkin's face implodes. "I don't know his name, and you don't either." He points a finger disapprovingly at Anya. "You don't know him. You hear me? You and Marty had break-down somewhere. Right? That's what happened. You had to get ride. Right? You don't know this maniac. Hear me? He was carrying things illegal and revolting. Police very interested to know if you two involved. Of course, you were not. You never even learned his name. All you did was sit in fucking truck. He nearly killed you both. Anyways I straightened most of it out with police."

Anya fidgets with the tubes by her arm. Underneath her bandages, she itches. She is sad she will not get to see Nancy.

"I stopped by site this morning too," Kupkin says. "They haven't been able yet to extract truck."

Joy floods Anya's face. She asks breathlessly, "The site where we went down the bank?"

"You could been killed," he says, "but somebody wants you to live."

Kupkin is a fatalist. He believes fate has determined that he rescue young women from around the world. He is also convinced it's preferable to their other choices.

Anya bubbles with excitement. "Mr. Kupkin, did you see a gray kitten?" She raises her hands even though it hurts. "Only this big," she says cupping her hands around an empty space. "A little guy but very spunky."

Kupkin sighs. After all, these girls are hardly more than children. "I wasn't looking, Anya." Considering everything else that has been lost, the thought of a kitten makes him laugh.

The excursion was altogether fruitless as well as unpleasant. The site was roped off by police tape, but no police were on guard. Kupkin and his chauffeur parked at the side of the highway, and because of the rain, slid most of the way down the embankment. The truck tires had forged a path through a stand of eucalyptus, then halted at an outcrop of rock. Several large trees were badly dented and the front of the truck smashed.

Near the truck were two bearded men, young hippie types. They carried a couple of ice chests.

"Police?" Kupkin asked them.

"Health department," they replied. "And you?"

"Forensics," Kupkin said.

They scrutinized him, the chauffeur, the limousine.

"Did you see a kitten?" Anya repeats.

"Even if I seen one, I'm not paying attention. Did you lose kitten, Anya?"

"I did," she says sorrowfully.

"There was this," he pulls out a packet of hundreds of letters. "For your *babushka*."

Anya holds the letters. She cherishes the letters. It is Ba alone who watches over her.

"And two hippies," Kupkin's eyebrow makes it a question. "You know them?"

Anya shakes her head.

Kupkin had gone to look for Marty's attaché case but found nothing in the cab except a bag of donuts, magnets with religious symbols, Anya's letters, and a few scattered clothes.

In the muddy track, he saw a half-buried blue eyeball in a plastic bag. He didn't believe it, but the chauffeur confirmed it was human.

"No wonder police so interested," he says. "Fucking truck was carrying eyeballs."

28

Anya dreads the task at hand. The last girl she oriented was Cerise, the girl once called Mary, now referred to as the Sepulcher. Anya counsels Cerise to ignore their jokes. Anya says they're only jealous because she has remained pure while they are rotten.

When Cerise first came from Romania, she was not only resistant but inconsolable. She cried. Day and night, she cried. For two weeks she never spoke and hardly ate. She made no friends and of course, was unsuitable for work of any kind.

In the beginning, all the girls face a terrible disappointment. They react with different emotions: anger, sadness, disgust. It's normal. They have been told that in America, jobs as waitresses, translators, even dancers await them. They feel betrayed by Mr. Kupkin. They have been lied to. Some suspect they've actually been sold by their family. They fault themselves for their own stupidity. They hate themselves and the mother who gave them life. They hate the deceptions of the world.

However, after a while, they adjust. They become resigned. It is hope that fuels this resignation. The hope is based on a difficult past that tells them nothing could be worse. Already when they come, they have developed a measure of endurance. They rely on endurance. They believe that once they complete their allotted time, they will be free. Not only free but unscathed. The layers of the past will recede. They will emerge with papers and money and begin their new lives.

Cerise was an exception. For a long time she had had no hope about anything. Her parents' death and years in the orphanage produced the misery of her existence. Her release into the care of Mr. Kupkin hardly affected her. She had no illusions about any bright future.

Once Cerise was in the States, she collapsed. She vowed to starve herself, make a quick end of it with a razor. She had to be isolated and constantly watched. It was an expensive confinement and bad for the morale of the other girls. Mr. Kupkin recognized he had to separate Cerise from the others. But it was counterproductive to leave her alone. She needed an empathic peer, someone seasoned.

Anya was driven to Atlanta from Charlotte. She and Cerise were housed in a suite at the corporate office. Meals were brought to them. Otherwise, they were left alone. Anya treated her apprentice like a daughter, despite the few years' difference in their age.

"All you have to do is let men touch you." She placed a hand on Cerise's arm. "Like this," she whispered into the girl's white childlike ear.

Then, Anya delivered her irrefutable perspective. It was a perspective she well understood. Would she rather be fucking a dog in Atlanta? Or living like a dog in Romania? For Anya, this was not a theoretical question but a real choice. The relative improvement of Cerise's plight could not be more clear.

At first, Cerise only cried. She had an inexhaustible supply of tears. But Anya was indulgent. They bathed together. They ate together. They sipped brandy and smoked. They cuddled and watched movies. After a couple of days, Cerise's crying subsided.

"See, it's not so bad." Anya was delicate, firm, and affectionate. "I'm certain it was worse for you before. That's why we cry. We cry like babies when we come. We do not expect it. Most of us have not imagined it. Most of us are shocked even if we were sluts at home. At least, at home if we did something for a gift or money, we could pick and choose. But here," she swept her gaze over the plush surroundings. "Here we learn to grow up and become women."

Cerise confessed that she didn't like to be touched. The contact of a stranger's skin made her cold. Worse, it made her lonely. Instead of connection, it reminded her of separation. In the orphanage, no one hugged or kissed her. She was never touched at all. She counted this as her only blessing since other children were frequently raped. She had been spared because she had a protector. It was the protector whom Mr. Kupkin paid.

"But does it feel so bad?" Anya whispered, kissing, caressing, and touching her. "It only feels bad if you resist. When you surrender, it is bearable. When you relax, it is almost sweet. Try now to relax. Try for me."

Although Anya had the incentive of $3,000 credit, coaching reluctant girls is infinitely harder than fucking. It requires intimacy. It requires intense human engagement. To be successful, you have to dig for a wellspring of hope. Hardest of all, you have to get emotional too.

By the end of a week, Cerise was resigned. She was depressed but willing to work. As Anya pointed out, the sooner she got busy, the sooner she could leave.

Everyone was happy with Anya's success. The night Cerise lost her maidenhead, the company grossed a fortune from spectators alone.

Now there's another girl. Marty has guaranteed that once this orientation is successfully completed, Anya's debt will be officially terminated. She will be given identity papers, her Green card, and $5,000 in cash. She will walk out unaccompanied.

29

After lunch, two visitors appear on Anya's floor. They are young with neatly combed pony tails. They wear jeans, work shirts, down vests, and expensive sneakers. They could be students or clerks in a record store. One carries a bouquet of mixed flowers.

"We're here to see," they stop at the nurse's desk.

"We don't know her name."

The other interrupts, "A Russian girl who came in yesterday."

The nurse scans the list of patients. The only possibility is Zoya Chobina. She was admitted without identification after the truck where she was a passenger dropped over an embankment west of the Caldicott tunnel. Her guardian, Dr. Kupkin from Atlanta, has been with her all morning and arranged with the hospital to put her under his care. The police too have stopped in. Apparently, the driver of the truck tried to outrun the police. At least, that's the rumor.

"Our friend is in love with her," one of the men says.

"We brought these to cheer her up," the other holds up the flowers.

"Five minutes," the nurse eyes them skeptically.

"And what's her name again?"

"Zoya, 408."

Kupkin is not in the room. He has gone back to the Claremont for a massage and hot mud wrap at the spa. When the strangers knock and enter, Anya is dozing.

"Hey," one of them kicks the leg of the bed.

Anya opens one eye.

"You remember me, Jimmy? My friend, Phoenix?"

Anya does not. She stares at the bouquet.

"Wrong room," she says weakly.

"We don't think so." Jimmy tosses the flowers on the bed as if it were a grave.

Anya doesn't like their looks. She reaches for the buzzer to the nursing station.

"No need to call," Phoenix says. "We checked in at the desk."

Anya turns towards the window. The pale rain drums the glass like the paws of a kitten.

"Mohammed? Remember him?"

"What's happened to him?" she asks anxiously.

"Deep shit, man," Phoenix responds.

Anya focuses on the wall. Mohammed was meant to be her savior.

"He cared about you," Jimmy says. "He told us."

"Yeah, if anything happened to him, man, he wanted us to watch over you."

Anya swallows several times. She is thirsty. She doesn't want to cry. Under the sheet she squeezes the web of skin between her thumb and finger. Someone once taught her she could stop pain if she squeezed a certain point. It's painful to squeeze, but it distracts her from the real pain.

"The money, we need it now for Mohammed."

Anya turns to the two men. There is a flicker of recognition.

"Money?" she asks innocently.

"Don't play us, man," Phoenix says without emotion.

"Mohammed's money."

She shakes her head.

"You see, it's really our money." Jimmy slaps Phoenix's back. "Him and mine."

"Mohammed's crazy. Mohammed fell in love with you at first sight. That's how he is. Mohammed is a lover. We know what crazy lovers do."

Anya shakes her head.

"They give their money to their bitch. That's what they do."

"Mohammed loves you so much, man. Maybe he gave all of it to you to keep, right?"

"I never," she tries to speak.

"It's our fucking money, man," Phoenix repeats.

"Maybe the police," she offers.

"Police don't know shit," Jimmy's voice lowers in a threat.

"They don't fucking got it, man," Phoenix adds.

"Mohammed don't got it. It's not in the truck. We walked all over the mud. That leads us to conclude."

"I never saw," Anya starts to whimper.

"You saw plenty," Jimmy says. "It's written all over you."

"Tell us, man," Phoenix grabs Anya's wrist and starts to wind it like a clock.

"Don't," she cries.

"Think about it. Think about Mohammed and how much he loves you."

"Love at first sight, man."

30

Anya is placed in a wheelchair and rolled downstairs to Kupkin's limousine. Ten minutes later, the driver carries her upstairs to the newly renovated apartment house on Lake Merritt.

Kupkin intends to make Oakland a deluxe center for the best girls and the highest-paying clients. It's the first phase of his new expansion plans. He expects Oakland to attract wealthy Pacific rim clients from Hong Kong, Singapore, Japan.

Each of the six spacious studios has been painted a salmon color. The fabric for the spreads, settees, and chairs is a leaf pattern that goes well with the salmon. There are teak chest-of-drawers and end tables. Spy-holes, video cameras, tape recorders have been installed in the units behind large prints of Oriental erotica. Against fire code, locks have been placed on the outside of each door. Instead of painted windows, there are heavy brown velvet drapes. Inside the airy studios are new king-size beds, new quality sheets, new expensive towels.

The short journey has exhausted Anya. She collapses onto a bed in pain.

"Rest," Kupkin advises. "That is all you can do. Ribs will heal properly with rest."

"I won't be able to manage by myself," Anya says.

She wants to tell him it was better in the hospital. At least, she was not alone. She had Nancy and the other nurses. Someone came to check on her, clean the floors, and bring her meals. Inside the bare hospital room, she could almost be herself. She was relieved of Kupkin and his managers watching over her, monitoring and bothering her. She was relieved of the smells and soiled bedding. Her imagination and memories were free. She could almost feel she was a normal girl.

"I flew in L.A. team," Kupkin says. He lowers his voice, "Help you get well and watch over Tuzla."

"She's here?" Anya is surprised.

Kupkin points to the wall that divides them from the next studio. "I thought you work on her here, but of course only after you get little better."

Anya is puzzled by the arrangement. "It's so open, so accessible," she says.

"She made havoc in Atlanta. I had to get her out of there. Since I already scheduled to come here, I brought her along. Once we officially open, only top girls come here." He regards Anya tenderly. "Girls like you."

Anya's eyes narrow viciously. As far as she's concerned, she will soon be unavailable.

"As a courtesy, traveling customers can use studios twenty-four hours a day. They can use conference room and office upstairs for business. And girls too."

Anya thinks back to her first year of confinement. She rarely saw daylight. Nothing was brand new, nothing freshly painted.

"After what Marty told me, I'm surprised you'd bring her here."

"The only way I manage is barbiturates." Now Kupkin thinks as a last resort, he will shoot Tuzla full of heroin and drop her off in West Oakland. Or East Oakland. Or Richmond. Some desolate place where there's an OD everyday.

However, heroin is against his policies. Kupkin forbids the use of heroin. He doesn't want his girls turned into zombies with smack or maniacs with coke. He wants them willing and alert. He has built up a clientele who expects a certain responsiveness. Live action.

However, if the girls are well-behaved and inclined, they are permitted a limited supply of marijuana and alcohol. They can receive sleeping pills for insomnia, ibuprofen for headaches and menstrual cramps, Aciclovar for herpes, serotonin up-take inhibitors for depression, and controlled doses of methadrine for fatigue, overweight, and low productivity.

Anything other than common ailments are treated by the company's private doctor, including abortions. Although he only completed two years of medical school in Guadalajara, he is their doctor. The girls trust him.

"Is Tuzla sleeping now?" Anya asks.

"All time sleeping. She gets shot every four hours."

After a perfunctory knock, a man enters. It is Drago, one of the managers from Los Angeles.

"Where's Anya?"

Kupkin points to the bed where the covers have nearly swallowed Anya.

"So you tried to kill Marty or what?" Drago chortles.

Drago is a tall, bulky Croatian who wears only velour jogging suits and polished white Addidas. He is a man who makes a joke of everything, but hardly anyone laughs. He is lewd, and his jokes are stupid.

Marty and Drago are polar opposites: one too soft, the other too harsh. In a way, Anya prefers Drago's intractability. Then, you know where you stand.

The worst thing about Drago is he takes advantage. Managers aren't supposed to mess with the girls, but Drago does. He prowls around, looking for someone to fuck during off-hours. He's nasty about it too. He always wants to do it in the ass. However, nobody complains. Once after someone complained, Drago used her exclusively for a month. He wouldn't let her rest. She suffered permanent damage to her bowel.

"I brought you friend," Drago says cordially.

Off-hand, Anya can't recall any friends. Maybe Mohammed or Nancy felt like friends for a few hours.

"You gonna thank me."

She rolls back to the wall. She can't stand Drago, especially his voice. When he speaks, his words sound as if they're stuffed with mucous. She wishes the earth would open and swallow him and Mr. Kupkin. If it swallowed her, that would be all right too. It would make her feel noble to sacrifice her own life for the end of theirs.

"What about earthquakes?" she suddenly asks. "Aren't there earthquakes here where everything falls down?"

"I was fucking chick in Northridge earthquake," Drago reports. "We was thrown, the two together like Siamese twins from bed to floor. I thought I was going to lose dick." Drago laughs, of course. "I thought ceiling was going to crash on top of me. Or crash through floor. Or windows breaking all over place and cutting me up. Or wires dropping down on building and starting fire. You ever been in fucking earthquake? Everything shakes. Everything in world makes noise. You hear noise and feel shaking and think world coming to end. They tell you get under doorway or table. But you too scared to move. Or if you move, then you want to run. They tell you that exactly wrong thing to do. But you want to get out of building into street. That ain't so smart. There are flying poles, flying bricks, falling wires, all shit on street crash down on you too. You think you want to run away, but it's earth. You can't ever run away from that."

"Shut up," Kupkin whispers sharply.

Drago's mouth clamps. His big melon head hangs apologetically.

"Go across street and get us sandwiches. Pepper turkey on rye, mustard, no mayonnaise, lettuce no tomato, bar-b-que chips, low-fat milk." Kupkin turns to Anya, "What you eating?"

Anya shakes her head.

"I want you to eat, Anya. You need to eat because already you have problem with your weight. You scrawny, Anya. You went and got too skinny. We don't want you skinny. You don't look good like that. Your face too thin, makes your skin bad. It's jaundice color, your skin. You need to put meat on your bones. Bring her roast beef sandwich and potato chips too."

Anya protests. "I'm a vegetarian now."

Kupkin chuckles. "You aren't anything, Anya. You aren't anything unless I tell you. Vegetarian? Where you get these kind of ideas? Vegetarian is for two kinds of people, Anya. Either you grow up believing you not supposed to kill things. Like Hindu in India. They don't kill cows, but they kill Pakistanis. So what that tell you about vegetarians? Anyways I know you, Anya. I know where you were raised. You're not fucking Hindu."

Kupkin laughs. Drago echoes him.

"As for other kind of vegetarian, it's somebody who thinks meat bad for you. Like something wrong with it. You know how many people starving around world? You probably don't know number, but you used to be one of them. They starving for meat. Meat is what everybody wants. Meat absolutely best thing you can eat. Like nice car for your body. You can't live right without it."

"I don't like the taste of meat," Anya complains.

"You totally in wrong fucking business then." Drago cracks himself up.

"I'm not in the business," she whispers.

"Look at me," Kupkin orders.

Anya lifts her chin, but even eye-to-eye, Kupkin can't make contact. Anya's eyes are sealed.

"Marty told me when I finish with Tuzla, then I'm through."

Kupkin claps his hands and smiles good-naturedly. "Marty told you that?"

"He showed me his books. He told me with my bonus for Tuzla, the account should be even. I won't owe anything anymore. He said I could leave from here."

"And hospital bill?" Kupkin sobers. "What about that? Is that on house?"

"How much was it?" Anya despairs.

"Maybe $5,000," Kupkin says. "Maybe more. Things add up rapidly in hospital. That's why I brought you over to apartment. I thought you appreciate nice atmosphere. And save yourself money. It's pretty here, isn't it?"

Anya's head folds into her chest. Maybe they don't plan to let her go. Maybe she's been too good, too easy. Maybe Marty told her those things to make her like him.

"We not going to talk about it now. After you get well, we look over bills, then we talk about it. It just another thing for you worry about now. Worry you don't need, meat you do."

31

When Drago returns with lunch, Cerise is with him.

Cerise is the big surprise. She has come with Drago from Los Angeles. Dressed in white, she is as pale as ever, white and translucent.

Cerise glides over to the bed and hugs Anya's arm. "You hurt?"

Anya moans. Pressure anywhere puts pressure on the ribs.

The two men have gone to the next room to check on Tuzla. Once Kupkin returns to Atlanta, Drago will be in charge. Drago is pleased with the assignment. Oakland has a human scale. The small residences, the old brick churches, the cluster of office buildings, the distant sparkling white courthouse, the lush green park, the playground, the families of ducks on the lake remind him of Yugoslavia before the war. He is glad to be on vacation from Los Angeles.

"I heard Marty's bad," Cerise says.

She leans against the pillows next to Anya and grasps her hand. There is a close sisterly feeling between them and precious few occasions to express it.

"They don't know when he'll wake up," Anya says. "Or what he'll be like when he does."

"I'd rather be dead," Cerise predictably concludes.

She'd rather be dead than anything else. In fact, Marty recently put her on anti-depressants. He thinks it's unwholesome for someone so young to be so hopeless.

"Mr. Kupkin says his brain might already be dead, but his body is still alive."

"Exactly the opposite of me," Cerise says.

She lovingly strokes Anya's hand. She would do anything for Anya. Sometimes she thinks Anya is the only reason she hasn't died.

"Marty made me leave without telling you good-bye. I told him I wouldn't go, but he said I had to. He said he was going to fine me. I thought that was all right. I would take the fine if I could stay longer to make sure you were safe. But then, Marty punched me. He knocked me out."

"I knew we'd see each other," Cerise says dreamily. "They didn't want to bring me here, but I can't work. Somebody complained he got a yeast infection in his mouth so they're going to let me rest up."

The two young women lie silently. The curtains are open, and the blue winter twilight and gray chips of clouds spread over the lake.

"I think I should go back to the hospital," Anya finally says.

"You feel bad?"

Anya rolls her eyes over the ceiling to indicate they shouldn't speak freely. She studies the room, trying to locate the hidden recording devices and video camera. The far wall is a picture window of double-pane glass, and the other three walls are covered with reproductions of Japanese paintings. The men and women are clothed in beautiful kimonos except for their genitalia which are oversized, exposed, tumescent. Anya assumes the microphones and lens are behind the framed prints.

"If I can get back to the hospital," Anya mumbles softly, "there's somebody who might help us. She gave me a feeling, a caring kind of feeling. She's my night nurse."

Cerise is skeptical. For over a year, she has been perfectly obedient. She is unsure what help signifies. She certainly doesn't trust it. When Galina got caught trying to run away, Kupkin called the I.C.E. authorities. Galina was deported back to the Ukraine.

Before deportation, Galina requested political asylum. She said there were no jobs in the Ukraine. She would certainly be forced into street prostitution. She informed I.C.E. about Kupkin's operation, but after one visit to the corporate offices in Atlanta, the investigation was closed. Galina was not credible.

From time to time, Kupkin and his managers remind the girls what awaits them in their home countries. If their family members are alive, most likely they will not be welcomed back. They will not only be a disgrace but a disappointment because they will come back as poor as when they departed. Their return signifies total failure for the entire family who has depended on them to help bring them to America too. Their distant life in America inspires the family's only fantasy, and their reappearance signifies the end of it.

Cerise won't do anything if it risks deportation. Almost none of the girls will. Some of them never want to leave. They like the familiarity, the security. Any unknown frightens them. They feel uncertain about work on the outside. They feel unfit for other kinds of relationships with men. They've disconnected themselves from genuine sexual longings. They recognize they've been ruined. Cerise has finally concluded, like most eventually do, that anything is better than going back.

On the other side of the wall, something smashes on the floor. They hear a shriek, followed by a command from Drago.

"The new girl is crazy," Anya says. "As soon as she got to the States, she went completely mad. They keep her drugged."

The two girls tune their ears to the commotion. A body slams against the wall. Short, breathless yelps from the girl alternate with Drago's hoarse commands.

"Shut fuck up," he yells.

Skin slaps skin. Their bodies hit the wall again. The framed picture next to Anya's bed falls to the floor. Drago continues to grunt, but the woman's voice is suddenly mute.

"Stop it!" Anya bangs the wall with her palm.

In the next apartment, an alarmed Drago stops for a second. But his grunts quickly resume in between a stream of curses.

Another breakable shatters.

"Stop it!" Anya continues to shout.

She cannot throw her body around. It's too painful to lift the lamp or vase. Instead, she picks up one of her spike heels and taps it on the wall.

Drago's grunts are a torment. Either he has killed or gagged the crazy girl.

"Stop it!" Anya sobs.

She looks to Cerise to help her, but Cerise is incapacitated. She has fled the bed. She is huddled in the farthest corner of the room where her head is covered with a pillow. Hugging herself with her arms, Cerise rocks back and forth on her heels like a miserable child.

Anya pounds the bottom of her heel on the wall. She cries out for Drago to stop. If only she could hear a sign of life, a yelp or shriek from the crazy girl. But she hears nothing but Drago's groans of satisfaction.

32

As soon as Kupkin enters the building, he hears Anya's shouts. Two at a time, he mounts the steps to the third floor. He unlocks the bolts to Anya's apartment. One of the expensive Japanese prints has fallen to the floor.

Next to the wall, Anya is holding a chair for support. In one hand she clutches a shoe. She is sobbing, banging the shoe's heel against the freshly painted wall. Small, round, dark impressions mark the salmon-colored surface where the heel has indented the sheetrock.

Kupkin wheels around. Cerise's face is buried in a pillow, her torso trembling.

He takes several furious steps towards Anya, grabs the shoe from her hand, and shoves her to the bed.

Anya blinks her tear-soaked eyes. Looming over her is Kupkin's apoplectic face. She chokes when she tries to speak.

"You need somebody to get something?" he bellows, grabbing her shoulders and shaking her.

Anya's head rolls on the top of her spine. She is about to faint.

"What you need?" He shakes her until she cries out. "Fucking vegetables to stuff your face?"

"No, no, no," Cerise aspirates. Her own voice has never sounded so loud. She jumps up and runs to Anya's side.

"She actually speaks," Kupkin seethes. "And what does she actually say?"

Cerise blushes. She is usually silent, white and silent which is why they call her the Sepulcher. She points to the wall of the next apartment.

"Drago," she says.

Kupkin rushes out one door through another.

"You pig!" He yanks Drago's huge half-naked body off of Tuzla and dumps it on the floor. He kicks Drago in the groin. His English shoes are heavy leather. Drago rolls to the floor. "Fucking son-of-pig," he continues to cry and kick.

Drago covers his penis with his hands. His slab of face is red, sunken. His cheek is deeply scratched in parallel lines, and the lobe of his ear is bleeding.

The room is a disaster. Glass is shattered over the parquet floor and rugs. The mirror is smashed. Two of the walls are cracked.

Tuzla lies face down on the bed. Kupkin rolls her over. As soon as he removes the gag from her mouth, she starts to yelp.

"I can stuff back in," he says coldly.

Tuzla pulls a blanket to her neck. She does not want a gag or shot. She puts her fist inside her mouth to control the yelps.

Kupkin walks back to Drago. He kicks him in the rib.

"Pig," he mutters again, but this time it is not so forceful. He does not approve of violence. When circumstances necessitate violence, it gives him no pleasure. It exhausts him. He is fond of saying that violence is never a win-win situation. He regards it as a personal failure. When he occasionally turns to religion for solace, he counts it among his sins.

Tuzla lies rigidly still. Her yelps diminish, then subside, but every fiber of her body remains tense, waiting for the next assault.

Tuzla doesn't understand. Kupkin's behavior confuses her. It appears Drago has done something wrong. She doesn't understand because Kupkin has repeatedly told her to expect strange men to have their way with her. But now this brute, who called her a "Bosnian whore" and tried to force his way into her ass, is in trouble.

And who are the others? A few minutes ago, she heard a woman shouting through the wall.

"Clean this up," Kupkin orders Drago.

Drago crawls to his knees. He adjusts his jogging pants around his waist. He touches his cheek.

"Look what she did to me," he whines. He begins to put the larger shards of mirror into a pile.

"Why she scratch you?" Kupkin is on the verge of exploding again.

"No reason," Drago stutters. "That's what I tell you, she didn't have any reason."

"You must been close enough for her to strike."

Drago's mind is working to gather an explanation.

"Close but only looking," he whimpers. "I thought she sleeping. You told me," he accuses, "drug makes her sleep five, six hours. I didn't think she wake up."

"And so?"

"So I crept there," Drago whispers. He now has the chance to plead his case. "She sleeping. I want to check her out."

The two fix their eyes on Tuzla.

Her head rests against the pillows. Her body is covered by a blanket. Fatigued, hung-over, depressed, and terrorized, she is still beautiful. She looks illuminated from within. Her skin is rosy gold and her hair golden-blond coils. Her face glows like a little child.

While the men stare in admiration, the yelping sound inadvertently mounts in Tuzla's throat.

"She so beautiful," Drago says helplessly.

"So beautiful you had tie her hands, put rag in mouth, roll her over, pull pants down, and stick in her?"

Kupkin is furious again.

"No, Mr. Kupkin. That not what's happened."

"She pulling your pants down and begging you?" Kupkin pokes a finger into Drago's sternum.

"No, Mr. Kupkin. It wasn't that. I got close to her but looking only. Look, don't touch. Mr. Kupkin's Golden Rule. We all know rule."

"Our business is finished here." Kupkin checks his watch. "There's flight to Los Angeles every hour."

"I was over by bed. But then," Drago continues, "her eyes flashed. They opened and flashed," he stumbles for a word. "They blinded me when they flashed. I lost balance. I fell forward. When I got close, she took advantage. She raked fingernails across my face."

Apparently, Kupkin is not impressed. "You can go back tonight."

"But she attacked me, Mr. Kupkin. She crazy person. You told so yourself. She attacked you too."

33

Kupkin slips into a chair next to Tuzla's bed. He has called Seattle to send in Drago's replacement. In the meantime, he must sit and wait.

With Cerise's help, the room is somewhat tidy. Except for bits of glass buried in the rug, it has been swept up. The prints have been put aside. They will have to be reframed and the walls repaired.

Every time Kupkin considers the expense, time, waste, and repeat of effort, his blood nearly boils. All his fury is directed at Drago. He wonders how he could have ever trusted him in the first place. Drago had been in the Army's special forces during the Bosnian war. He escaped retribution, prosecution, and immigrated to the States.

The FBI recently visited J.P.K. in Atlanta with a subpoena for Drago. It was issued under the Torture Victims Protection Act. Kupkin admitted to authorities that Drago had been employed as a restaurant manager but left the company six months ago. Kupkin lied to the authorities. He participated in obstructing justice for a pig.

Once again, Tuzla is drugged and sleeping. Cerise bathed and fed her. Afterwards, Kupkin gave her another shot.

Anya is sleeping too. According to the doctors, Marty's condition has not changed. However, the police returned his attaché case and gun. The van, owned by J.P.K International, has not surfaced. Nor has Pedro, living or dead, been sighted. At nine o'clock, Drago was sent with Cerise by taxi to the Oakland airport.

Outside, a single string of tiny white lights encircle the lake. A mist has settled over the water, and the lights look like floating pearls. Kupkin stares at the lake, the joggers, the lights.

He has a terrible headache. From time to time, he experiences moments of despair. He thinks he has failed. He doesn't know what or whom. He only knows there's a sinking feeling in his chest. He can't tell whether it's physical or emotional. He has asked the doctor if it's his heart. The doctor is reassuring. He believes it's nerves and recommends Kupkin cut back on coffee and take more vacations.

Kupkin recalls that this jaunt to the West Coast was slated in part for recreation. For this too, he blames Drago. And Marty. And Tuzla. All of them.

If the weather improves, he may drive to Carmel for a little winter tennis. The thought enchants him. He was only in Carmel once, and he loved it.

On the bed Tuzla sleeps fitfully. She tosses and talks incoherently. Kupkin studies Tuzla's face. Inexplicably, a photograph of Marilyn Monroe's broad, animated derriere flits through his mind.

"The soul of a woman lies in her ass," he used to like to say.

Anya's behind is too narrow for his taste, but it doesn't matter. Not everyone is like him. One client even asked if he could marry Anya. It would be a financial exchange. A transfer. Kupkin told him he'd think about it.

Like any natural wonder, Tuzla is perfect as is. However, it is nearly certain this face, this perfection will prove more bother than it's worth. After all, it is Tuzla who has initiated the entire series of troubles. Tuzla is bad luck, and while not Kupkin's first mistake, she is his biggest. Nonetheless, it continues to be unclear what exactly is a feasible or desirable outcome. In business, especially negotiation, it is important to ascertain the desired outcome before discussions begin.

Inside Kupkin's chest the hollow, empty feeling persists. He searches for the pulse in his neck. It's racing. He relaxes his hunched shoulders, folds and stretches his fingers, rotates his stiff wrists, and presses his temples.

He tries to speak to his body about serenity. He tries to recite a Buddhist chant his wife taught him. She assured him these unintelligible syllables could help eliminate suffering. He can't really remember the chant. He has to make it up. He repeats, "Calm yourself" over and over in several languages.

The power of suggestion is effective. His pulse slows. His chest opens and expands, and the sad, lost sense of self dissipates. Even the throbbing pain diminishes. Once again, he is clear-headed. He enumerates his successes. Real success by any measure, he tells himself.

However, as soon as he directs his attention to the question of the girl, the uneasiness and nervous pulse return. A casualty of war, he concludes. Beyond saving.

34

K upkin taps his chin while he speaks to Anya. "We can't keep her drugged all the time," he says. "Awake, she's impossible." "I haven't seen her," Anya says.

"You fall in love when you see her," his voice rises excitedly. "She is too beautiful. She should be film star or something. But it's too much responsibility." He hesitates. "I thought it could work out."

"You ought to let me try. Remember how difficult Cerise was at first?"

"Cerise is depressive. She's unpleasant but not threatening. This one's different. This one tiger. She's untamed and demented."

"Patience," Anya says.

"I have only so much patience." He lifts his pinky finger.

"I have much."

"I'm sure you rather do something other than usual. For you, Tuzla extends vacation. For me, she's hell."

"You ought to let me try," Anya begs. "That's why we came here. At least, I should get a chance to try."

"You see trouble she has caused simply by lying in bed? You, Marty, Drago, van, Pedro, truck with eyeballs, the accident, police. It's catastrophe." Kupkin ruminates. "It's Tuzla. She's bad luck."

Anya dips back into her bowl of Chinese noodles. She has come to believe in Tuzla as a liberator. What is bad luck for one person is good fortune for another. She'd just as soon be on the other side of luck from Jean-Paul Kupkin.

"Sometimes the worst piece of luck makes everything right," Anya says. She is thinking of her cousin. After her aunt's apartment was blown up in Moscow, her cousin was adopted by a rich family in New York.

"Eating vegetables softens brain, Anya. Bad luck is always bad. That's how life works."

"You ought to give me one chance."

"I know what you think, Anya. You think success with Tuzla will wipe books clean. I'm not sure where you get this idea. You tell me Marty showed you books. But Anya, look at me. You've only been four years here. Nobody pays off debt that quickly. I don't care if you fuck like two bunnies. It takes maybe five years when you owe so much. And hospital bill add something too."

"I can't do it anymore, Mr. Kupkin." Tears submerge Anya's calico irises.

"Do what, Anya?"

Anya has lost her nerve. She can't say.

Kupkin turns back to the lake. The hour is late. The streets are quiet. The faint calling of a strange noise chirps in the distance. It bleats two alternating but continuous songs. One like a hollow cuckoo and the other, almost a suction or gasp.

"What's that fucking noise?" Anya asks. The same one haunted her in Los Angeles. Now it has followed her north.

"It's stop light at intersection. When light changes, tone changes so blind people know when to cross street."

Anya listens. The two tones have now penetrated the silence. They are all she can hear.

"It drives me nuts." She laughs sadly. "I fantasized it was a bird."

Anya thinks she should have felt sorry for the bird, but instead she hated it. Now that she knows it's for the blind, she hates it still. She wonders if she is a bad person. She doesn't think she was born bad, but life has turned her. She has even lost pity for the blind. Maybe Mr. Kupkin is right. Maybe bad luck is all bad. She wonders if a bad person can someday be good again.

Kupkin turns on the radio. "Better?"

It's the news, but anything is better.

"Do what, Anya?" Kupkin reminds her.

Anya has nearly forgotten.

"A few minutes ago, you said you can't do it anymore. I was unsure what you meant."

Now he's playing. Anya can see he's playing. Of course, he knows what she means. If anyone would know, it's Mr. Kupkin.

"I don't think," she struggles on bravely. "I don't want to have sex with strangers."

"Want?"

"I mean I don't think I can."

"You mean you don't like your job?" Kupkin asks without irony. "Lots and lots of people don't like their job, Anya. This is life."

"Yes, but then they quit. They get another job."

"You think people just quit? Most of time, they don't have choice to quit. Most of time, they can't just quit. They can't just find other job. They have responsibility, family to support, legal obligations, debts. In your case Anya, you have all of these. Your family depends on money we send them. You know about your contract obligations. And we already discuss debt."

"But isn't there something I can do? Something else?" Anya races on. "I'm smart, Mr. Kupkin. I'm a quick learner. You could find me work at headquarters. I could help you with sales. Or type on the computer. Or be a hostess. I could help with the girls. You know if you wanted, you could find something else for me to do." She pleads.

Kupkin taps his chin thoughtfully. He waits to answer. "In principle Anya, you're right. You are smart. You learn fast. But this is also true of work you already do for me. Clients love you, Anya. They want to come back to you again. You think they feel same about Cerise? Cerise is dead meat to them. She has no personality. She has no life. But everyone loves you, Anya. They love everything about you."

Kupkin pauses to gather his most important point. "I have to think about business. Always I have to think what is best for business. Who to put where, this is complicated. This is what makes business hard."

Anya stirs the noodles with her fork. She wishes Mr. Kupkin would return to the next room. She would like to rest and listen to the radio. She wishes Cerise would come back and keep her company. Even

Cerise's silence is a comfort. When Cerise finally speaks, she says things she has thought about for a long time. She says things that are unexpected.

Unlike Mr. Kupkin. Everything he says is expected. He bores Anya. She wonders if it would surprise him to know how boring he is. She wishes she could tell him, but he intimidates her. He carries an air of power. He's the lawmaker, the king. He moves around as if he owns whatever he touches. When someone destroys what he owns, like Drago or Tuzla, then he metes out the appropriate punishment. For Drago, banishment. For Tuzla, drugs.

"There is one thing I can think of," Kupkin smiles mysteriously.

Anya is almost afraid. The possibility of choice frightens her. He has bothered to trouble himself about her. She's not sure if she likes that. It bestows him with a quality of consideration, possibly kindness. It means he doesn't want her to be unhappy. Most importantly, it underscores his real power. If he wants to, he can change her life.

"I thought of something," he says now with certainty.

"What?" Anya is unsure.

"Big personal favor to me."

Anya wonders what kind of favor Mr. Kupkin would want from her. She wonders if he has a secret sexual predilection. He has strict rules about messing with his girls. He encourages his managers to marry and leave the girls alone. He himself never shows any indiscretion.

"Very personal," he repeats. Kupkin usually doesn't permit the use of the word. He likes to remind the girls their job is impersonal, sex is impersonal, their bodies are impersonal.

"And once it's over, our business is finished. Like Marty promised, we clear books. We make it final. You can leave with papers, Green card. They are in Marty's attaché case. You can have bonus."

Anya flushes with surprise. This is unexpected.

"So?" He is smiling in a friendly, intimate way. "Do I have your promise?"

Kupkin locks and unlocks his fingers. Business is sometimes an unpleasant affair. The unpleasantness does not come easily to him. He shrugs with distaste. "For papers, for clearing of debt, for bonus, one favor."

35

Anya holds the blue gun, Marty's gun. Like a fine car, it has both mass and grace. Weighty enough to be reliable, light enough to wield.

"It's simple thing really," Kupkin releases the safety. "What does sleeping person feel of death? Don't we say person is blessed when they die in sleep?" He secures the safety and points the gun to his heart, "Here."

Anya's own heart suddenly thumps underneath her ribs. She tries leaning over, but it hurts too much.

"Less messy than head," he says.

"One bullet, that's all it takes?" Anya balances the gun on her palm. Marty never let anyone touch it. Now she has it in her hand. To hold it is to possess it. "What if someone hears?"

"Building empty, Anya. Under renovation. No one here."

"I'm scared, Mr. Kupkin."

"Yes, but you are also brave."

"It doesn't take courage," Anya counters.

Kupkin disagrees. He believes a terrible kind of courage is required to kill another human being. "What does it take then?"

"I don't know," Anya cries. "I really don't know anything about it."

Kupkin lifts the gun from her hand and puts it back on the console. "It's up to you, of course."

Anya scrutinizes the man's small, shapely head, the silver highlights in his well-trimmed hair, the gloss on his recently manicured nails.

She remembers that Marty once told her when you reach the top of the food-chain, you never have to clean up your own shit.

"What if I can't?" Anya asks. The gun makes her giddy. She's afraid if she pulls the trigger once, she will go around shooting the whole world.

"No problem. I was only trying to think of equivalent. You know what I mean?"

Anya shakes her head. She does not know the word.

Kupkin picks up the gun and one of Anya's shoes. "This maybe worth $40 new." He holds out the shoe. "This gun $2,000. Not equivalent." He removes his watch and holds up both gun and watch. "These are worth same. These cost same. However, I prefer to have watch. It's more useful to me. Also, I prefer because it's peaceful." He smiles, pleased with himself.

"Blow-jobs cost more than hand-jobs. They are not," Anya carefully enunciates, "equivalent."

"Precisely, but that comparison directly relates to time. It's straight-forward. One hour more costly than thirty minutes. However, true value is not strictly driven by cost. Also, there is factor of taste. For me watch has value gun does not. For Marty, the reverse. You, for example, probably care more about shoes than watch or gun." He calculates. "But if I was you, I choose gun. I sell it and then with money, buy hundred shoes."

"So the equivalent of everything I owe is Tuzla's death?"

"Exactly."

Anya wonders if that means Tuzla's life is worth a little or a lot. When she last tried to see her brother in jail, the police told her he wasn't worth it. She didn't understand what they meant. She still doesn't understand. At least, in the case of the police they had a pre-text to hate her brother.

"I can't possibly look at her."

"Of course not. I will cover her face with sheet or towel before you come in room."

"She'll look dead then, Mr. Kupkin."

He sits and folds his hands together. He has nothing else to say. Either Anya will kill Tuzla or not. He has done what he can to persuade her.

Anya's eyes volley back and forth between the picture window and gun. She tries to think of herself as a murderer, but then she has never thought of herself as a whore. Most of the time, she thinks of herself as a foreign worker with a job in the United States.

She ogles the pretty gun. She doesn't have to oblige Mr. Kupkin. He even said so. She considers the consequences. She could be fined. Or demoted. She could be sent back to the lap-dancing circuit. If only she knew if the nightmare was ending or beginning.

"I can't possibly bend over," Anya says. She must keep away from any actual contact. "When?"

Kupkin checks his watch. "Before Seattle arrives in morning. Only you and I know then. That's better, isn't it? We don't need witness. Witness compromise things."

Anya's stomach rolls over. Reflected on the glass of the window are different colored eyeballs. Each one is suspended in fluid and packaged in a little plastic bag. Printed over the bags are red arrows that point down.

"If Seattle walks in and sees body, that's easy. Nobody minds dealing with body. Body is like taking out trash."

"Do you think I could have a little vodka?" Anya asks softly.

Mr. Kupkin nearly grins. A drink to him means a deal.

"We tell them black man broke in while we out to dinner. The black man shot Tuzla. No problem. Oakland's full of murders, full of black men."

He strides across the room to a small refrigerator. Inside are several brands of vodka. He picks Hangar One, carries it and two stubby bar glasses back to Anya.

"The Americans make good vodka," he says with humor. "They make this just down the street."

He pours two jiggers into one glass and hands it to her. He pours a child's thimble into his own and raises it. Anya speedily drinks the vodka without raising her glass.

36

A few minutes later, Anya and Kupkin tiptoe down the hall to Tuzla's room. When they enter, Anya gasps. The towel is not in place. It has slipped down to Tuzla's chest. Her face and neck are exposed. Her features, relaxed and composed. Her face is soft and inattentive. Her eyes are open and still like two blue pools. Her focus is distant as if she hasn't figured out where she is. Her long, dark lashes blink and brush rapidly against her sleepy-pink cheeks. She is not yet awake, but she is waking.

As soon as Kupkin comes to the bed, the softness instantly drains away. She tenses. A strained, high-pitched yelp rises in a gurgle inside her throat. But instead of yelping, she collects the last drops of moisture inside her mouth and spits.

Kupkin makes the awkward attempt at an introduction.

"This is Anya, Tuzla. I told you about Anya. Anya wants to help you." Kupkin clears his throat. "She is on the Adjustment Team."

Anya backs towards the door. She can feel the weight of the SIG inside her bathrobe. "Adjustment Team" is a very poor joke.

Kupkin retreats into the bathroom for another hypodermic.

Tuzla attempts to speak, but her tongue is thick from drugs and sleep. She fixes her entire concentration on Anya, searching for traces of empathy. Inside Anya's strange calico-colored eyes, she finds something frightened and vulnerable. Something familiar.

"Help," Tuzla whispers. The utterance sounds like the first word she has ever spoken.

Anya turns directly to the girl, face-to-face. Her fresh beauty and its imprint of fear remind Anya of her younger sisters, her home, her people. Around Tuzla wafts an aura. It surrounds her with a force other than human. Or perhaps it reveals another kind of human: a creature who has been captured, transported, abused, and drugged for the price of skin and meat. A slave.

However, the creature is more clever than the man perceives. She wants to survive. She fights to survive. She has cultivated the art of speech, and with this art, she begs one last time for help as Anya herself has secretly, silently begged.

Anya hates pity in all forms. Either to give it or get it. The world is too harsh to waste in pity. But now she cannot help it. Tuzla's helplessness rouses her pity. Although Kupkin has described the Bosnian girl as mad, defiant, aggressive, Anya sees nothing but innocence. She is the tormented princess of an ancient tale, subjected to the influence of an evil spell.

Anya turns from Tuzla's stare, her plea and helplessness. She feels herself getting sick. She wants to vomit. She limps to the toilet. She is not well.

"Give me gun," Kupkin demands.

Anya touches the weapon reluctantly. If she hands over the gun, she is powerless.

"Why?"

"Because it is mine, because I say so, because you don't have guts."

Kupkin is reminded of the secret to his success, to all worldly success he believes. It is the ability to do exactly what others avoid.

"Are you going to kill her then?" Anya trembles. She is moved to imagine heroics.

Kupkin holds out his hand for the gun.

"Maybe you can talk sense into her after all," he says. "I see how she looks at you." He smiles. "As Chinese say: *first thought, best thought.*" He pats Anya on the shoulder. "We go back to plan A. Gun?"

Anya lifts the blue wonder from her pocket. Shaking, she wobbles into the bathroom and grips the rim of the toilet with her hand. She slips to the cold bathroom floor. The cold tiles are refreshing. She touches her forehead. Perhaps she has a fever. When she vomits, there is a filmy stream of blood suspended in the water.

"Mr. Kupkin," she calls weakly.

There is no liberty for her now. Remorse and relief compete for her attention. She had a chance, and it was forfeited. Already long ago, she learned to mistrust the meaning of chance. Even before Mr. Kupkin. Or before her grandmother fell into a hole. Or before her brother was mistaken for a terrorist. Once she thought Mr. Kupkin was sent by the angel of good fortune, but what fortune did such an angel bring her?

Anya is too tired to sort it out. She hardly cares. It will soon sort itself. She will go back to fucking for J.P.K. International. Or die of an internal hemorrhage. Or be deported to Russia. Or pawned off somewhere somehow. Or Mohammed will recover and miraculously find her. The last possibility is the only one that pleases her.

Mr. Kupkin helps her back to the other suite. She lies down gratefully and drifts into sleep. She sleeps, and in her dreams there are shouts. There are men shouting.

"Mohammed's money," a man's voice cries out angrily.

Anya presses her ear against the wall. She can hear Mr. Kupkin. He responds coolly. He recognizes the pair from the site of the accident. "There is no money."

"Don't fucking lie to us, man. Everybody thinks they can lie to us."

"I know no Mohammed," Kupkin says confidently.

Anya can hear Tuzla yelping. She hears something heavy smash a wall.

"I am a medical doctor," Kupkin says. "We should all stay calm. Discuss matters calmly. Let me give her medicine first, then we discuss what you need."

The yelps do not stop.

"Shut up, shut up, shut up," Phoenix's voice repeats vehemently. A shot follows.

"Money the other bitch took," Jimmy says. "She took it from Mohammed."

"I know no Mohammed."

Two shots follow. There is a groan.

"Son-of-pig." That is Kupkin's voice.

Anya strains to hear through the wall. There is a commotion. Chairs and tables overturned. Something banging. A door opened.

"Look at fucking this, man," Phoenix says.

Anya thinks he sounds happy. She thinks he probably found Mr. Kupkin's large money roll. She hears them shut the door and walk through the hall. She hears the front door to the building slam.

There is silence. It is silent except the mechanical bird in the distance that sings when it is time for a blind person to cross the street.

37

Anya is frozen with fear, but she makes herself move. She knows how to make herself do things against her will. She limps into the bathroom, locks the door, and slips into the empty tub. She nuzzles against a towel on the slope of tub and wraps another towel tightly around her like a truss.

Then, she sleeps. She sleeps deeply. She doesn't stir. She doesn't dream. She sleeps like an infant inside the safe and trusted circle of someone's arms.

When she wakes, she wonders if Ba has been holding her. Her body is cramped, cold. Her ribs ache. She stretches out her limbs and strips off her clothes. She bathes and dresses in the clothes Nancy found for her at the hospital: the long, baggy rayon skirt, the plain denim shirt and gray woolen sweater, the pair of thick white socks, clogs, a ski jacket, and knit cap. She stuffs all her hair inside the cap.

She opens the bathroom door slowly. She walks to the next suite slowly. Her eyes light on Tuzla. She is in the bed, exactly as Anya last saw her. Tuzla's eyes are open, but now they are hollow. They are twin dark caverns. A look of rigid surprise immobilizes her face. Her lips are slack, discolored. Her smooth hands are folded on her chest. Her abundant blond hair cups her head like a fur bonnet. A single trickle of blood apologetically stains the pillow.

In front of the bed lies Mr. Kupkin. He has fallen on the rug as if he were running and suddenly tripped. His face is down. Anya cannot see his face, only the ruby blood that puddles beneath his chest.

The pockets of his lined raincoat are reversed. Marty's attaché case is on the table. The SIG has scuttled to the portion of parquet floor beneath the windows.

Outside, the sky is overcast. Joggers bundled in hoods and gloves run along the path around the lake. Anya can see the vapor of their breath in the chilly air. Across the lake, the branches of large, leafless trees sway in the wind. It must be early.

The doors to the new closet and refurbished bathroom are ajar as if someone left carelessly, suddenly. This is no reassurance they won't return, for it turns out that life is like a shark, dangerous and unpredictable.

Anya picks up Kupkin's raincoat and with its corner lifts the SIG from the floor and places it next to his body. She dumps Marty's attaché case. All the identity cards she finds for herself, she puts inside her own jacket pocket.

She walks indifferently over Kupkin's body to the bed. She stops to stare into Tuzla's face. Like so many wasted beauties, she thinks, Tuzla is dead.

Anya falls down beside her. She hugs her slender arms. She kisses her pale face. She combs through her hair with her fingers. She gazes into her opaque eyes, searching for a thread of connection between the living and the dead.

For an instant, Anya thinks she has found something still alive. Within that instant, she imagines meeting in another time and place. In school perhaps, as schoolmates. The older girl, Anya, is guiding the younger girl. Anya imagines their hands clasped and swinging as they skip down a street lined with tall houses. The street, school, town, houses, they are all intact. They have not been bombed or invaded. They have not been raped or abused.

Anya dissolves with emotion. The dead girl deserves to be mourned. At least that.

Anya is not a religious person. Her beliefs are vague. She believes in the existence of evil, and sometime long ago she believed in the existence of good. She believes that life is a trial. It seems as if almost every moment she is tried. She believes in her ancestors and something they believed has passed into her. There was a great misfortune, but she does not know how to describe it. She tries to remember the prayer her grandfather said when Ba died. She adds her own words, "Pray for your Anechka." She says, "Amen, amen, amen, amen" many times until it becomes a chant. She hopes it brings peace to Tuzla.

"Wasted," she cries, covering the face with a sheet.

Then, she closes the door to the apartment. She places Kupkin's raincoat around her shoulders. She limps down the stairs of the apartment house.

Out on the street, Anya looks in both directions. There are no workmen in sight. No police. She steps a few feet forward towards the lake. A friendly jogger nods his head as he runs past her. In the cold air, his breath mingles with hers. For an instant, the sky folds back on itself, and a ray of sun falls on the surface of the water.

At the corner there is a convergence. A few cars move around a circular boulevard in the direction of office buildings on the far side of the lake. A city bus grinds to a stop. A crowd of school children climbs the steps of the bus. A bicyclist waits for the light to change, and when it does, the signal for the blind changes tone.

Anya hears it as her signal too. She walks towards it.

At the intersection is a man who looks neither young nor old, white nor brown, fat nor thin. On his back he wears several coats, and on his head a scarf and hat. He stands waiting to cross the street. With him is a grocery cart, filled with his belongings. In the cart is an assortment of bottles and cans he has already collected from the neighboring garbage bins.

Anya recognizes him as a class of man. He is homeless, she thinks. He is a man who knows how to disappear. He knows how to make himself invisible. Disappearing, it is a form of magic. Along with the princess now dead and the evil spirit temporarily broken, the art of vanishing is contained in the ancient tales.

Anya stands next to the man, examining his rags. She moves closer to him. His hair is matted, but he does not smell.

The light changes, and he and his cart rattle onto the street, up the sidewalk on the far side.

Quietly, Anya follows. She would like to speak to him, to ask him for advice, but she will wait. For now she will simply follow, and if he wants to know what she's doing, she will answer that she is unsure.

Then, when she feels it's time, she will inquire where she can find such a cart, where she can find a sleeping bag and tarp. She will ask him to help her. She thinks that in this way, at least for now, she can remain safe.

THE END

a note about the type

Minion was designed by Robert Slimbach in 1990 for Adobe Systems. The name comes from the traditional naming system for type sizes, in which "minion" is between nonpareil and brevier. It is inspired by late Renaissance-era type.

Zelmont Raines has slid a long way since his ability to jook, to out maneuver his opponents on the field made him a Super Bowl winning wide receiver, earning him lucrative endorsement deals and more than his share of female attention. But Zee hasn't always been good at saying no, so a series of missteps involving drugs, a paternity suit or two, legal entanglements, shaky investments,and recurring injuries have virtually sidelined his career. That is until Los Angeles gets a new pro franchise, the Barons, and Zelmont has one last chance at the big time he dearly misses. Just as it seems he might be getting back in the flow, he's enraptured by Wilma Wells, the leggy and brainy lawyer for the team – who has a ruthless game plan all her own. And it's Zelmont who might get jooked.

"A hard-edged, wonderfully creative work
with the kind of literary bite that lingers."
–Robert Greer, author of *The Mongoose Deception*

"Enough gritty gossip, blistering action and trash talk
to make real life L.A. seem comparatively wholesome."
–Kirkus Reviews

"Gary Phillips writes tough and gritty parables about life and
death on the mean streets – a place where sometimes just
surviving is a noble enough cause. His is a voice that should be
heard and celebrated. It rings true once again in *The Jook*, a story
where all of Phillips' talents are on display."
–Michael Connelly, author of the Harry Bosch books

FRIENDS OF PM

These are indisputably momentous times – the financial system is melting down globally and the Empire is stumbling. Now more than ever there is a vital need for radical ideas.

In the year since its founding – and on a mere shoestring – PM Press has risen to the formidable challenge of publishing and distributing knowledge and entertainment for the struggles ahead. We have published an impressive and stimulating array of literature, art, music, politics, and culture. Using every available medium, we've succeeded in connecting those hungry for ideas and information to those putting them into practice.

Friends of PM allows you to directly help impact, amplify, and revitalize the discourse and actions of radical writers, filmmakers, and artists. It provides us with a stable foundation from which we can build upon our early successes and provides a much-needed subsidy for the materials that can't necessarily pay their own way.

It's a bargain for you too. For a minimum of $25 a month, you'll get all the audio and video (over a dozen CDs and DVDs in our first year) or all of the print releases (also over a dozen in our first year). For $40 you'll get every-thing that is published in hard copy. *Friends* also have the ability to purchase any/all items from our webstore at a 50% discount. And what could be better than the thrill of receiving a monthly package of cutting edge political theory, art, literature, ideas and practice delivered to your door?

Your card will be billed once a month, until you tell us to stop. Or until our efforts succeed in bringing the revolution around. Or the financial meltdown of Capital makes plastic redundant. Whichever comes first.

For more information on the FRIENDS OF PM,
and about sponsoring particular projects,
please go to www.pmpress.org,
or contact us at info@pmpress.org.

PM PRESS was founded in 2007 as an independent publisher with offices in the US and UK, and a veteran staff boasting a wealth of experience in print and online publishing. We produce and distribute short as well as large run projects, timely texts, and out of print classics.

We seek to create radical and stimulating fiction and non-fiction books, pamphlets, t-shirts, visual and audio materials to entertain, educate and inspire you. We aim to distribute these through every available channel with every available technology – whether that means you are seeing anarchist classics at our bookfair stalls; reading our latest vegan cookbook at the café over (your third) microbrew; downloading geeky fiction e-books; or digging new music and timely videos from our website.

PM Press is always on the lookout for talented and skilled volunteers, artists, activists and writers to work with. If you have a great idea for a project or can contribute in some way, please get in touch.

PM PRESS . PO BOX 23912 . OAKLAND CA 94623

WWW.PMPRESS.ORG